FYREA'S CAULDRON

Borgo Press Books by WILLIAM MALTESE

Anal Cousins: Case Studies in Variant Sexual Practices
Back of the Boat Gourmet Cooking (with Bonnie Clark)
Blood-Red Resolution: An Adventure Novel
Catalytic Quotes (Some Heard Through a Time Warp)
Draqualian Silk: A Collector's & Bibliographical Guide to the Books
    of William Maltese, 1969-2010
Emerald-Silk Intrigue: A Romance
Even Gourmands Have to Diet (with Bonnie Clark)
The Fag Is Not for Burning: A Mystery Novel
From This Beloved Hour: A Romance
Fyrea's Cauldron: A Romance Novel
Gerun, the Heretic: A Science Fiction Novel
The Gluten-Free Way: My Way (with Adrienne Z. Milligan)
The Gomorrha Conjurations: An Adventure Novel
The "Happy" Hustler
Heart on Fire: A Romance
In Search of the Perfect Pinot G! (with A. B. Gayle)
Incident at Aberlene: An Espionage Novel (Spies & Lies #1)
Incident at Brimzinsky: An Espionage Novel (Spies & Lies #2)
Jungle Quest Intrigue: A Romance
Love's Emerald Flame: A Romance
Love's Golden Spell: A Romance
Moon-Stone Intrigue: A Romance
Moonstone Murders: The Movie Script
Schism on Antheer-D: Science Fiction (Gods & Frauds #1)
Schism on Bnth: A Science Fiction Novel (Gods & Frauds #2)
Slaves
A Slip to Die for: A Stud Draqual Mystery
Summer Sweat: An Erotic Anthology
SS & M: Being Excerpts from the Nazi Death-Head Files
Total Meltdown: An Adventure Novel (with Raymond Gaynor)
When Summer Comes
William Maltese's Wine Taster Diary: Spokane & Pullman, WA
Young Cruisers

FYREA'S CAULDRON

A ROMANCE NOVEL

WILLIAM MALTESE

THE BORGO PRESS

MMXII

FYREA'S CAULDRON

FIRST EDITION

Published by Wildside Press LLC

www.wildsidebooks.com

DEDICATION

For My Dear Sister, "Pandora"

CONTENTS

CHAPTER ONE
NOT IN LONDON ANYMORE

"Purely of volcanic origin," Pierre Yonne said to Marie Camaux who stood beside him at the rail of the steamship as Saint-Georges Island appeared even larger on their horizon. "The Pitons du Daunet on the island's south side is all lava, or agglomerate masses, dating back to the Tertiary Period."

The one teacher in the lone, small school on the yet unsighted Isla Charlotte, Pierre was a storehouse of local information. A curious man could find plenty of things to keep himself occupied when he had a spare moment or two. He was headed back to work after a holiday to visit family and friends in the States, actually glad to have escaped his mother's constant badgering that he jettison his enjoyable bachelor life in favor of wedded bliss (or whatever).

"Quite different from what we saw at Bermuda," he continued. The liner had departed Hamilton, Bermuda, a few days before. "Bermuda is coralline formation, mostly white limestone, highest point only two-hundred-sixty feet."

"Certainly, this is all different from England,"

Marie said, feeling another splatter of sea spray against her face. Since she had reached warmer climes, her skin had taken on a decided bronze cast, although she couldn't help remembering all the tales of how exposure to the sun could age a woman overnight. Still, Charles had continually commented, in London, on how her peaches-and-cream complexion would be improved immensely with a little more color.

Charles Camaux was Marie's husband, and, if he liked her tan, who else mattered?

"Yes, I should imagine this is different," Pierre said, having never been to Europe for any first-hand comparisons, although he still had relatives in France—to hear his mother tell it. The Yonne family had come to the New World with Lafitte during the American Revolution and had set up house there ever since. Pierre's mother had actually considered her son an expatriate when he took up temporary residence on an island that was a French possession.

Marie felt a small lurch in the pit of her stomach as the ship changed course to begin a more pronounced riding of ocean swells. She hadn't weathered the sea part of her voyage at all well, getting sick off Port Johns and staying that way most of the way. At the moment, she could think of nothing less desirable than arriving on Saint-Georges even mildly under the weather. Charles would undoubtedly empathize, but she was looking forward to their reunion too much to have it spoiled by an upset stomach.

"Perhaps, you wouldn't mind my visiting you after

you're settled in," Pierre suggested tentatively, having already gathered from brief discussions that Marie was disembarking with literally no friends or acquaintances (save her husband), on the main island. Pierre, who occasionally made it over from Isla Charlotte, had always been curious about the Camaux family. He was even more curious now that its heir-apparent had gone all of the way to England for a bride.

"Oh, of course, do feel free," Marie granted, once again diverting her attention from the upcoming landfall to her attractive companion. More than once, she had regretted how her queasy stomach had kept her so confined to her cabin, since Bermuda, and unable to discourse with someone like Pierre who so obviously knew such a great deal about the area. Marie's knowledge of Saint-Georges, besides the quick cram-course she had attempted on the internet in the rush before departure, was thoroughly lacking. Charles had always been exceedingly vague whenever she'd questioned him.

"You will have plenty of time to learn all about the island and the Camaux family after you get there," Charles had said. "Until then, let's enjoy London, since I certainly don't know how long it will be before either of us is back here."

In the final analysis, Marie knew very little about her husband, Charles Camaux, except that she loved him. That certainly was enough for her, even if her mother had been frankly appalled at the speed of the courtship and the wedding.

"In my day," Carolyne Nelson had said to her daughter, having consented to the marriage only after friends had reported the Camaux family was *well-connected* at the Court of St. James's, "this type of shotgun proceedings would have caused more than a few raised eyebrows."

However, whatever the wagging tongues, if any, Marie would, at least, be far enough away so that they would make little difference. Obviously, Saint-Georges had its own social order, quite separate from that of the British capital.

"The harbor of Villeneuve," Pierre said, pointing to bring Marie's attention back to the growing landmass.

"It's bigger than I expected, "she admitted, seeing the rather extensive docking facilities now in the foreground, and the layers of pink and white houses that climbed the hills beyond.

"About fourteen-thousand, by way of permanent population, at the last census," Pierre informed. "Actually, the island's headcount increases substantially during the tourist season, although not as much as some of the more prime travel destinations in the Caribbean."

Yes, Marie had read that; so, why had she expected Saint-Georges to be one of those small atolls she could walk across in a day, instead of this three-hundred-square-mile chunk of densely forested lava rock? Probably, it had something to do with how the tellie programs were forever representing the stereotype tropical paradise with half-clothed natives, and meals obtained by machete from the nearest coconut palm.

"Well, I'm afraid I do have a bit of last-minute packing to do before docking at the quay," Marie said apologetically as the ship gave another shift to better align for entrance into the mouth of the harbor. "I do hope, however, you're serious about stopping by whenever you have the time. I'm afraid I'm not sure just where I'll be staying..."

The thought suddenly struck her that if Charles wasn't there to meet her, she wouldn't know where to go, or what to do.

"I'm sure I'll have no trouble tracking down the bride of Charles Camaux," Pierre said, giving hint that Marie had, indeed, been self-deprived of a veritable font of information by having been so often confined to her cabin the past few days.

"Then, I shall be looking forward to seeing you again," she said, allowing Pierre to take her right hand and squeeze it gently in parting.

In the rush prior to disembarkation, Marie didn't catch sight of Pierre again, although, on one occasion, she did look frantically for him when she felt suddenly certain her husband had abandoned her, leaving her to fend for herself on some Caribbean island a few thousand miles from the only people and places she had known all of her life.

In the end, her face beginning to go damp from a combination of panic and tropical heat, she saw Charles on the quay. She waved. He saw her and waved back. The flooding of relief that rushed through her at that moment managed completely to alleviate all traces of the sickness which had—even until then—lingered in her stomach.

Soon enough, Marie surrendered willingly into Charles' welcoming arms. The force of his strength took her breath away. The sudden press of his lips against hers, with such unexpected enthusiasm, was such a surprise in having, frankly, never been matched by anything he'd ever managed during their, albeit brief, London courtship.

Marie felt each and every line of his decidedly male body pressed against her: his muscled chest, flat belly, firm thighs....

"It's so good to see you!" he said, pulling back to look at her. His voice was deeper than she remembered. In fact, he was somehow different. Defining the difference was another matter. Possibly, it just had to do with the time, the place, and the circumstances. After all, this wasn't London. The brightness of this sun—seeming a totally different than what had shone down on them in England—gave the place a strange air of unreality.

Certainly, he *looked* pretty much the same: so, it apparently wasn't any kind of glaring physical anomaly that Marie sensed. His skin was burnished a deeper bronze than she remembered, making his blue eyes even bluer, but his jaw still had its characteristic squareness, his mouth its sensuous fullness, and his cheeks their distinctive dimples that balanced the deep cleft in his chin. His neck was still bullish, ending in the hair-covered vee of skin that appeared at the open collar of his white shirt.

"Give me your baggage tabs, and I'll have the bags loaded while we have a bit of refreshment at the hotel," he said, his eyes sparkling in a way that was uncharacteristic of the rather serious and somber Charles whom Marie had known in London. Then, it was only natural he should be more at ease on his own stamping grounds. "Did you have a good trip?"

"I'm afraid I'll never make a good sailor," she admitted.

He laughed. His lips slipped easily back to reveal his wide expanse of white teeth. He took her left arm in his right hand and exerted the pressure necessary to guide her through the crowd. They stopped briefly while Charles transferred her baggage tags to a Negro man introduced as Petre. Then, Marie and Charles got into an awaiting taxi, the driver apparently having received previous instructions as to their destination.

The Hotel King Philip was a confection of pink architecture situated on a small rise overlooking the harbor. As it was only a short drive, Marie had only just gotten settled into the cab before its door was again open, and she was stepping back into the bright sunlight.

"Monsieur Camaux," a white-liveried Negro on the porch greeted as Charles came up the stairs. He turned dark black eyes on Marie. "Mademoiselle."

"Madame Camaux," Charles corrected.

The Negro got a decidedly strange expression, and, then, turned to lead the couple down the porch to a small table in the shade. There was a good view of the steamer still disembarking its passengers and baggage on the quay.

"I believe there's a bottle of *Pouilly-Fuissé* waiting us on ice," Charles told the black man before turning his attention back on Marie.

"I couldn't possibly drink much wine, Charles," she protested. She feared a resurgence of her queasiness.

"We'll just have enough to keep us in good spirits on the long drive home," he assured her.

His use of the plural, by way of who would be drinking, thoroughly confused her. She had never seen him take one drink of alcohol. At the beginning of their relationship, she was sure he had said he was a teetotaler.

"Oh, I see!" Charles exclaimed, suddenly, as if it dawned on him as to how he was seemingly acting out of character. "You must learn that the Charles you knew in London isn't quite the same as Charles, here, on Saint-Georges. Or, do you object to your husband occasionally having a nip or two?"

"Of course I don't object." Marie had been raised in a family where wine with the meals was de rigueur, and she could embrace this unexpected turn of events. She had usually foregone wine when with Charles, rather than drink it alone.

"Good," he said, settling back in his chair and eyeing his wife as if he were really seeing her for the very first time. "Now, tell me all about your trip.

She began a brief rundown of all that had occurred

since their last meeting, keeping a close watch to make sure her story wasn't becoming too boring. The wine arrived just as Charles' interest was peaked by Marie's mention of her brief encounter with Pierre Yonne.

"From Isla Charlotte, you say?" he asked while the waiter filled their glasses.

"He said it wasn't too far from here."

"Oh, it's not. Just half an hour by sail."

"I hope you didn't mind my telling him he might call. He's really about the only passenger I had a chance to speak with onboard."

"Of course I don't mind. I'm just curious as to what he might have had to say about our marriage."

"Not much of anything, really. The longest conversation I had with him took place just shortly before we docked. That consisted of his commenting mainly on the island topography. I think he said he was just returning from a sabbatical of some kind in the U.S."

"There is a small school on Isla Charlotte, now that you mention it," Charles said. "So few people, though, on that dismal little rock pile, these days, that you'd think the whole lot of them would have packed up their bags and come back here after over eighty years of waiting, wouldn't you?"

"Pack up their bags and come back? Waiting for what?" Marie had been struck by the obvious oddness of Charles' phraseology.

"Paranoid lot," Charles observed, sipping his white wine. "Most of the original bunch went over in 1931. No one wanted the place before then. Now, I guess, their children's children are still taught to expect another blowup from The Cauldron at any minute."

"The Cauldron?"

"You must have seen it when you sailed in," he said, filling their glasses with more wine from the bottle he retrieved from the ice bucket after waving off the waiter. "It's always the first of the island to be seen on the horizon."

"Mont d'Esnembuc?" Marie distinctly remembered the emergence of that domed-shape mass, seemingly from the sea.

"That is what it's called on the maps." Charles worked the wine bottle back into the ice. "Around here, it's simply The Cauldron. I guess a few million years back, there was a collapse of the central part of the mountain, during an eruption, to cause the sizable lake now up there. You'll enjoy a day trip, by horseback, for a look-see. You do ride?"

Marie tried to decide if Charles was joking. Twice, they had borrowed horses in London from the Galen-Waydes for trots through Hyde Park bridle paths.

"Then, every English girl rides, doesn't she?" He flashed a wide smile and reached across the table to give her hand an intimate pat.

She was going to answer with something. She didn't know just what—but something. She had this inexplicable feeling (had since that first unexpectedly passionate kiss on the quay?), that, somewhere between London and Saint-Georges, Charles had undergone several definite changes.

"Ah, our car!" he said, nodding toward the limousine which had reached the upper curve of the hotel gravel driveway and was pulling to a stop. "If we hurry, we can reach the Château for an early supper."

CHAPTER TWO
INAUSPICIOUS BEGINNINGS

"Charles, are you all right?" Marie asked. Actually, it was Marie who wasn't feeling well. Her seasickness of the past few days was replaced by car sickness brought on by the twisting road the driver chose immediately upon leaving *The Hotel King Philip* driveway.

"I'm feeling fine," Charles replied, giving Marie a loving pat on her leg. "I must say, you're looking rather peaked, though."

"Would it be horribly inconsiderate of me to have the driver pull over to the side of the road for just one moment?" She was dreadfully embarrassed.

"I should have booked us into the hotel for a night to let you get your land legs," Charles apologized.

"I'll be fine," Marie assured. "Really, I will."

"I guess I was just anxious to get you off to the old homestead," he said. "Forgive me?"

"If we could just stop for a moment?" She still tasted white wine long after it should have been beyond tasting.

"Of course." Leaning forward to tap the Negro driver on the shoulder, Charles said, "Petre, pull off at the next advantageous spot, will you? Mrs. Camaux and I would like to stretch our legs."

"I am sorry, Charles," she said. "I'm sure I'll be completely fine as soon as I get stopped for a couple of minutes."

"I imagine you still haven't adjusted to the heat and humidity of our little island, either," he commiserated; actually, the car's air-conditioner made Marie somewhat chilly. "Besides, the topography, made hinky by ancient lava flows, never allowed our roads, as you've noticed, to be built directly from any point A to point B."

The car rounded another bend and eased off the road onto a space that provided a spectacular view. The just-traveled highway was a ribbon of pink asphalt, appearing and disappearing amid stretches of flower-specked greenery. In the far distance, Villeneuve, all pink and white, slipped gently down to the harbor where the liner still rested at the quay.

"Feel like getting out?" Charles asked, once the car was completely stopped.

"I feel rather ridiculous, making such a fuss," Marie said. "I really don't quite know what's gotten into me."

How was she to know she'd react this way? Aside from a couple of summers in Spain (she'd gotten sick, then, too), she'd never been all that far from home.

"There's nothing about which to feel ridiculous," her husband assured, opening the car door. "This road often gets to the best of us."

He began circling the car to let Marie out, but Petre

beat him to it.

After the air-conditioned interior of the automobile, the outside would have been unbearable if not for a breeze blowing up from the sea. As it was, Marie found the temperature quite pleasant, although she was conscious of how her blouse had grown disconcertingly damp beneath her arms.

"Welcome to Saint-Georges, Mrs. Camaux," Charles said, standing close, and placing his right arm around her in a way that was sensuous in its familiarity.

Suddenly, she defined what had been so exceptionally unusual about their kiss on the quay. In London, he had hardly ever been affectionately demonstrative in public. Here, however, there had not only been the kiss on the quay but the way he had leaned to touch her hand intimately on the porch of *The Hotel King Philip*. Now, with Petre watching from a position by the side of the car, Charles' arm pulled Marie even closer.

She glanced up at him, somehow embarrassed to find him unabashedly returning her stare.

"You're very beautiful!" he said, his voice low.

Marie's blush increased. Why? This was her husband, merely having provided a simple endearment. Yet, it affected her as if it were coming from a complete stranger.

What was getting into her?

"I'm feeling much better," she said, guilty when she pulled free of his hug. Nervously, she glanced to see if he was hurt by her inexplicable rejection. He was eyeing her with what appeared to be genuine amusement.

"Then, we shall be on our way," he said and made no move to touch her as they walked back to the car.

Petre opened the door for her. Charles went around to the other side and crawled in. Ten minutes later, he was pointing out an exceptionally attractive roadside growth of purple-red bougainvillea, and Marie was, again, fighting a losing battle with nausea.

Possibly sensing Marie's return of car sickness, Charles limited his conversation to an occasional query as to whether or not she wanted to stop, again, for a few minutes. Finally, however, without his having put in any verbal request, the car, again, pulled to the side of the road.

"Let's take a moment or two," Charles suggested, as if he had anticipated this particular pause; which he had. "We can see the Château from here."

Petre came to open the door, and Marie stepped out. Charles exited and came around to join her. This time, however, he made no move to touch her, and Marie found herself missing his physical support.

"There!" he said. His arm outstretched toward a distant clearing amid the abundant greenery that covered one lower mountain flank.

Marie saw an obviously large lawn, beyond which was a quadrangle stone structure with an impressive square tower at each corner. There were large windows that caught sun and reflected it like spider eyes. A broad flight of steps, and a classical pediment, each provided a gracefulness and grandeur. From a closer perspective, the edifice undoubtedly would be even more impressive. Constructed of granite from the very mountain upon whose leveled slope it sat, the building was partially mirrored within a large adjoining reflecting pond. The source of the water was a stream, visible to Marie only as an impressive waterfall that tumbled a breach in the greenery farther up the mountain: the mountain dwarfed everything.

"Home!" Charles announced a strange smile playing at the corner of his sensuous mouth.

At that moment, Marie was mainly concerned with the road that remained, twisting and turning, between her and the estate. She might be seeing her new home, but she definitely wasn't there yet.

"Cacao," Charles said. His extended arm indicated a stretch of vegetation growing three sheltered mountain depressions within their immediate view. "Coffee farther up the mountain. Most of the natives live in quarters through those trees over there. You'll, of course, get a better idea of the layout after you've been here a few days. The stables are in the rear of the Château grounds. The lake within The Cauldron is up that way."

Marie's gaze followed the slope upward to where green became lost in swirling gray mist. She saw no sign of visible paths through the far tangle, suspecting it would be very easy to become lost on this island she had originally misconstrued as merely a wee speck of sand in the Caribbean.

"I imagine, by this time, you're ready for a nice hot

bath, yes?" Charles said, his mouth actually breaking into a wide smile.

His eyes seemed to be stripping the clothes from her body—like a man who hadn't yet seen what was underneath. The sensation brought goose bumps to Marie's flesh, and sent strange inner warmth racing to flush her cheeks.

"There are hot springs when you get rested enough to become more adventurous," he continued. "Better let me point those out to you, though. There's one in particular that has the nasty habit of going from ninety degrees to boiling within virtual short seconds, and I'd hate to have my wife become stew like one poor soul once did."

Marie would have laughed if she had known for sure Charles was joking. However, the Charles whom Marie knew—had known—hadn't shown much by way of a sense of humor.

"I'll point that to-be-avoided pool out to you the day we head up The Cauldron to see the lake," he promised. "We can catch fish in a stream but a few feet away, and, then, boil them in the thermal pool for a nice lunch."

Marie followed her husband back to the car, trying desperately to put together more of the little things which made him different than she remembered.

Despite all of her efforts to be rid of it, she continued to have a niggling premonition that something wasn't quite right.

* * * * * * *

Someone had possibly spotted the car when it had stopped at the lookout overlooking the house, because the staff was outside in full force to meet the new mistress, Mrs. Camaux. The surprisingly long line was headed by a wrinkled old woman whose age defied estimation.

"Look what I've brought, Little Mother," Charles said, a firm hand having guided Marie to a position directly in front of the female gnome.

Small black pupils stared out at Marie from a wrinkled face that looked more wizened monkey than human.

"Charles has told me so much about you," Marie said. That was a lie. Charles had told her nothing about this woman whose position in the household was made obvious by her prominent placement at the head of the reception line.

The old woman said nothing. Except for a slight dilation of her pupils, she showed no indication whatsoever that she'd heard Charles or Marie.

Marie felt ill at ease. Apparently Charles felt only amused, because he laughed and, then, nudged his wife onward to pause at the next person.

Marie would remember only one seemingly friendly face among the crowd that day: Karena, the fat Negress cook. On the other hand, she experienced no blatant hostility, either, except from Charles' mysterious "Little Mother". Mainly, the servants were distantly respectful as Marie so often found the well-trained help to be in aristocratic households. A couple of the youngest girls, apparently not long in service, had smiled shyly to excuse poorly executed curtsies.

"I thought you would prefer selecting your own personal maid," Charles said, guiding Marie through the impressive entrance hall to a larger room dominated by a walk-in fireplace and walls hung with animal trophies brought back from the far corners of the world. Anyway, Marie could secretly hope no similarly fanged live beasts were presently making their present homes in the jungle around the Château

"You'll have your pick of any girl from the village," Charles continued. "Or, if you'd rather not go through the tiresome bother of training one of the locals, I can have someone, already trained, sent in from Villeneuve. Either way...."

He trailed off in mid-sentence; apparently, he realized Marie still felt the aftereffects of her boat trip and car drive.

"There's plenty of time for all of that," he said after a moment. "For now, we'll have Madeleine show you your rooms."

He put his arm around Marie: the first time he had touched her since she had shrugged him off earlier. This time, she left his arm where it was.

Would you prefer I have Karena prepare a cold plate and a little white wine for you to have upstairs?" Charles suggested. "I assume you're too tired to go through the rigmarole of formal dining your first night, here."

"I'm going to be much more presentable tomorrow,"

she promised.

"Of course you are," he said, leaning to give her an affectionate peck on one cheek. Simultaneously, he motioned for the young servant girl who had been waiting on the sidelines to show Marie Camaux up the grand in-house staircase to her rooms.

* * * * * *

The bath relaxed her. Her glance in the full-length mirror assured her that she was visibly none the worse for wear. Obviously, youth was resilient; although, at twenty-six, Marie realized she was no longer a child. Still, her breast remained firm, her waist thin, and her legs long and shapely.

She selected a ruffled pink negligee, far sexier than one she would have chosen if she'd made the selection prior to her lengthy soak in the tub. She was even able to devour, with considerable gusto, the two cold chicken sandwiches that arrived with a carafe of cool white wine.

She was tempted to ask Madeleine about the hostile little old lady, but she didn't, probably because Marie was reluctant to confess not knowing the answer already.

By the time she had swallowed the last tasty morsel, she had revived sufficiently to contemplate going in search of her husband. She had a bit of apologizing to do, not because she had failed to respond like a seasoned traveler, but because she had let her imagination begin all sorts of fanciful flights. Why had she found it so strange a man was different, in his natural habitat than in foreign surrounds? After all, there was little similarity between England and Saint-Georges, although possibly the Château would have been more at home in France.

However, Madeleine, apparently assuming Marie would be going directly to bed, turned back the blankets, revealing clean white sheets. The vision proved so inviting, Marie surrendered all plans for anything save the comforts of the large supporting mattress.

She was no sooner in bed than she was asleep, waking some time later to darkness within which Charles sat the edge of the bed next to her.

"Charles?" she asked, extending a hand; he took her fingers and gave them a comforting squeeze.

"I didn't mean to disturb you," he said, his voice a whisper.

"Are you coming to bed?" Marie asked, suppressing a yawn. The bed continued to be seductively comfortable, retaining the warmth from her body. She was quickly being enticed back into complete lethargy.

"I just stopped in to check on you before going to my rooms," he said.

Marie was struck by the sudden realization that she had been assigned a suite separate from that of her husband. Although, why it had taken her this long to figure that out was beyond her. It should have been obvious from the absence of male toiletries in the bathroom, and the absence of male clothing in the closets (quite aside from the decidedly feminine décor of the rooms), that Charles stayed elsewhere. Marie didn't know if she liked the arrangement of not. She had always imagined a man and wife sharing the same bedroom—certainly the same bed, especially before the newness of matrimony wore off. For all intents and purposes, their marriage hadn't yet technically progressed beyond its honeymoon stage.

"Come to bed. Here," she invited, patting the bed clothes directly beside her.

"We need you rested for tomorrow, don't we?" he said, his smile evident even in the dimness. He leaned over and placed a tender but erotic kiss against her slightly parted lips. Rather than appease her swelling passions, his kiss merely added to them.

"Please, Charles," she said, taking her husband's arm as he obviously began his move to leave her. "Come to bed."

"What would your husband say?" he asked, gently disengaging her fingers from his large left bicep and continuing to his feet.

"My husband?" Marie asked, genuinely confused. She was positive she'd misheard. "Charles, you're my husband."

"Oh, but you're mistaken," he said, moving through the shadows to the door, gone before Marie was fully cognizant of his having left her.

For a brief moment, she thought she had been dreaming and still was. After all, the conversation of which she'd just been a part couldn't possibly have taken place; it was too bizarre? Obviously, it had been nothing more than a figment of her exhausted mind and body.

Yet, she wasn't asleep. She was sure Charles had been there on the bed but moments before.

She threw back her covers and came out from underneath them. She found her slippers and worked her feet into them before coming to a standing position. She reached for her robe which as thrown over the back of a nearby chair.

She followed Charles' route, opening the door to the sitting room.

The old woman was waiting for her in the darkness, blocking the path that would have allowed Marie access to the hallway. The sight of the gnome-like shadow within deeper shadows brought Marie to a sudden startled stop, a small gasp of shocked surprise escaping her lips.

"What are you doing here?" Marie asked, using her right hand to pull her robe tightly shut across her neck. "What do you want?"

"Why did you bring him back, you little fool!" the old woman asked, disgust evident in her voice. "You've brought disaster on us all!"

"I want to see my husband," Marie said, indignant that her voice should come out sounding like that of a chastised child asking for her father.

"He doesn't want to see you," the old woman said, not moving from her position. "Go back to bed!"

Marie tuned, went back into the bedroom, and drew the door sharply closed behind her. She was breathing hard. She could hear herself panting, the rhythmic expansions contracting her chest. She could hear the throbbing beat of blood in her ears.

What right did that old woman have to be in Marie's rooms, bossing Marie around? Marie was mistress of Château Camaux! She didn't know by what authority the old crow got off telling her what to do.

In a sudden flush of anger, at having been cowed by someone half her size, she once again opened the door to the sitting room. If she wanted to see her husband, then she would see him! If anyone tried to stand in her way, then that person could very well be expected to get shoved to one side.

The sitting room was empty. The spot once occupied by the old woman now held only a patch of moonlight which had managed to enter through a small breach in the drawn curtains.

Marie quickly crossed to the door, opened it, and stepped out into the hall.

The corridor was empty and silent. The whole house seemed mysteriously empty and silent.

Marie got a blood-chilling shiver that left her feeling icy. She stepped back into the sitting room and shut the door behind her. She quickly surveyed her surroundings, thinking, perhaps, the old woman was still there. There was only furniture, moonlight, and shadows.

Imagination? Was that what it had been? Was that *all* it had been? Had Charles really been at her bedside? Had she really followed him to be confronted by the old woman standing in this very room?

Another chill shivered its way along her spine. She went back to the bedroom and climbed into her bed, finding the sheets completely absent of any consoling warmth she might have left there.

It was a long time before she could find the peace of mind to surrender the strangeness of the night to slumber.

CHAPTER THREE
INEXPLICABLE..."THINGS"

Morning was something Marie felt rather than saw. After all, the room was still dark behind drawn curtains; the house was as silent as a tomb.

She didn't feel rested. So, maybe it wasn't morning after all. Maybe her senses played tricks on her.

Her eyes were sticky with sleep that came free on the backs of her rubbing hands. Her mouth was dry. She had a headache.

Her sleep had been fitful and spread through with dreams mainly unremembered...except for her husband, sitting on the edge of her bed...except for the old lady standing guard in the sitting room like Cerberus at the gates of Hades.

It took Marie several minutes to get oriented. She kept wondering where she was. This definitely wasn't England, or the plane, or the ship.

She threw back the blankets and came to a sitting position, dropping her legs over the edge of the bed. Without looking, she worked her toes into her slippers.

She picked up her robe en route to the French doors, fastening its cord before pulling back the curtains. The sudden entrance of light temporarily blinded her. Her right hand came to her forehead to offer shadow.

It was morning, but only barely. The sun, low on the horizon, only managed to reach the glass through a unique breach among the distant trees.

Marie was about to exit onto the small balcony, beyond, when the figure appeared beneath her and headed off across the lawn.

It was Charles, walking slowly, a bouquet of flowers in one hand, apparently completely unaware he was being watched. Reflexively, Marie, somehow feeling guilty in spying, stepped to one side so she'd be less likely seen by him should he chance to glance her way.

She wondered why she didn't just proceed with unlatching the glass doors in order to call out to him, in that that seemed the more logical thing for her to do. Surely, he would much rather greet his wife than proceed on any early morning stroll?

Still, she intuitively sensed he would be less than pleased were he suddenly to be made aware of his wife's Peeping-Tom status directly above him.

Marie couldn't help feeling like a spy. That was silly, wasn't it? What could possibly be suspect about her husband out on the lawn? Heading from where? Heading to where? For whom were the flowers?

She pulled back farther, unconsciously taking hold of the curtain to edge it more closely back into the position it had maintained throughout the night.

Charles continued across the grass, veering right toward the trees that bordered the long rectangular lawn on that side.

Movement in the shadows formed by the trees! There was someone there. Someone was waiting just within the border of darkness dividing the lawn from the thicker underbrush.

Charles stopped, obviously seeing the figure, too. Were the two talking? If so, no voices traveled to Marie, if just because the shut French doors kept out all such sounds.

The figure moved imperceptivity; just enough so Marie could identify the old hag from Marie's bad dream (not a dream?) from the night before.

Charles continued forward, stopped on the very edge of the forest, looked down on the old woman who was pathetically dwarfed by his powerfully impressive physique.

What was he saying? What was the old woman saying? What mysteries had driven those two to that specific spot, on that particular early morning, while the rest of the household was possibly assumed asleep?

"Oh!" Marie exclaimed, turning toward the unexpected sound behind her, her heart leaping into her throat. She felt a combination of guilt and embarrassment as she saw that her cry of alarm had so scared the entering Madeleine that the girl had dropped a vase of flowers. Several *habernia fimbriata* had ended up scattered across a water-spotted rug, one orchid stem awkwardly bruised and bent.

"Oh, Madeleine, I'm so sorry," Marie said, seeing the girl's wide-eyed expression complete with soon-to-be released tears. Marie felt solely responsible for the accident. If she hadn't been up and spying, but, rather, been in bed, where she should have been, none of this would have happened. "I'm afraid my nerves are just a little on edge, lately."

She went to her knees and began picking up the flowers, continuing a running one-sided conversation she hoped would convince the girl that Marie wasn't going to beat her for clumsiness.

Finally, Madeleine's horror at dropping the vase was replaced by the horror of Marie busy doing the cleanup in which Madeline should have been the one engaged.

"Oh, Madame, do let me do that!" Madeleine said, hurriedly grabbing up the last flower from the rug and depositing it in the luckily undamaged vase Marie, also, surrendered to her.

"Well, it looks as if the two of us have sufficiently rectified any damage, doesn't it?" Marie said with a wide smile.

Madeleine looked a little dubious as she noticed a sizable watermark on the rug, by the doorway, but Marie gave additional assurances, watching as the young girl finally deposited the salvaged vase and flowers on a bedside table.

Nonchalantly, Marie moved back to the window, noticing neither her husband nor the mysterious Little Mother any longer standing along the border of the lawn.

* * * * * * *

Charles entered while Marie was having breakfast in the dining room. He was obviously surprised to see her.

"I thought for sure you would prefer breakfast in bed, this morning," he said, coming around the table and picking up a hot muffin from the serving counter. He reached Marie's chair, bent, and kissed his wife gently on her right cheek.

"Had you witnessed how much time I spent in my bed during the voyage here, you might well understand my reluctance to stay bedridden now," Marie commented.

"Feeling quite refreshed, then, are you?" he asked. Then, before she could answer, he informed a servant he would merely be joining his wife for coffee and a muffin, since he had eaten quite a large breakfast earlier.

Coffee cup in place, the last of his blueberry muffin eaten, he turned his full attention on Marie.

"I feel much better, thank you," she told him. "Actually, I'm quite anxious to get out and about. You mentioned the lake in The Cauldron."

"Well, that does, indeed, sound like a complete recovery," he said, flashing an attractive smile. "However, I might suggest a few minor forays before we undertake such a major one. I'm afraid both of us will have to roll out of bed a lot earlier than this to make it to the lip of The Cauldron and back by night-fall."

"Quite far, is it?" Marie asked, although, by that

point, her question was obviously superfluous.

"I wouldn't want to exhaust you completely after one such marvelous recovery," Charles said, sipping his coffee and covetously eyeing another muffin on the service table. "I have to check the lower east valley this morning. Purely routine. I shall be perfectly free this afternoon, if you're up to a look around of the grounds."

Marie, who would have preferred a ride immediately after breakfast, surrendered to the fact she would obviously have to spend some time getting down the routine of the household. Certainly, she couldn't expect Charles to handle domestic supervision now that he was married.

I'll have Marc show you around the house, Charles said, anticipating the tangent his wife's thoughts had taken. "Don't worry too much about getting the hang of things too fast. This house has been without a mistress for...."

His eyes went suddenly glassy. His unfinished sentence made the resulting silence pronounced. His right hand began a slow drumming on the tabletop.

"Charles, are you all right?" Marie would have been up and out of her chair, or at least calling a servant, but his spell (or whatever it was) was short-lived. He shook his head, as if to clear it, gave a grin of embarrassment, as if he knew he'd been caught at something not quite normal.

"I'm quite all right," he told her, pushing back his chair and coming to his feet. "I was telling you not to worry too much about the chaos, wasn't I?"

"Something like that."

"Just remember to be firm with the staff," he said, coming around the table to plant his second affectionate kiss of the morning on his wife's cheek. "The heat spawns a good deal of laziness, but, on the whole, you'll find most of our people much more energetic than their peers in the villages and city."

"I'll try to keep that in mind," Marie responded with a smile. What she really wanted, she realized, was for Charles to take her upstairs to bed. However.... "You said you'd have Marc show me the ropes?"

Marc was the black butler. Thank God, Marie wasn't going to have to endure any early-morning powwows with the little old lady. She had no immediate desire to confront the old hag with the inappropriateness of that crone having invaded Marie's sitting room in the dead of the previous night. Although in the light of the morning, Marie wondered if the old woman could really have forbidden her to follow Charles into the hallway. Whatever had taken place last night obviously occurred while Marie was suffering from acute physical and mental exhaustion.

"I'll have Marc stand by for as soon you finish breakfast," Charles said, making his exit. He returned, momentarily, pausing long enough to thrust only his head back into the room. "Have Karena fix a picnic lunch. I'll get back early enough to enjoy it with you. Okay...?"

Before Marie could react with obvious pleasure, Charles was gone.

* * * * * * *

The management of the household was far from the chaotic state Charles had insinuated. In fact, everything seemed exceptionally well-oiled. Marc seemed pleased, in a very formal way, when informed by Marie that she really had no intentions of making any major waves in standard routine. She did make a request for a formal meeting with each of the servants (excluding the old lady). During the meetings, she took myriad notes, jotting down little things, like how they were two Helenes on the premises. Old Helene, not really old at all, except when taken in comparison to Young Helene, a girl of fifteen.

Julie, one of the parlor maids, proved the most talkative, dropping all sorts of household gossip, once Marie had skillfully broken down the girl's reserve: Rolphe, one of the gardeners, was supposedly sweet on Sylvie; Julie preferred one of the stable boys, Theodore; Karena, the cook, had a husband and five children, with hopes, although not yet having broached them with Mr. Camaux, of her eldest daughter eventually being brought into household service.

Julie proved such a storehouse of useful information that Marie was shocked when she realized it was almost noon. She hadn't yet informed Karena there would be the need for a picnic lunch for two in only a matter of minutes.

She began her discussion with the cook, however, by asking about whether Karena knew of the availability of any local girl Marie might train to be a personal maid.

"I would certainly prefer looking to someone whose references could be vouched by someone already in the household, rather than bring in some complete stranger," Marie said, remembering the conversation had earlier with Julie about the existence of the cook's eldest daughter. As expected, Karena immediately jumped at the bait. After Marie agreed to interview Karena's daughter, the next morning, she, only then, glanced at her watch and delivered an exclamation of well-acted horror. She followed with the confession to Karena that Marie had completely forgotten about the picnic Charles had suggested for their lunch.

The picnic basket was ready by twelve o'clock.

Originally, Marie had had intentions of possibly promoting Madeleine to the post of personal maid, but Jannette (Karena's daughter) obviously came with the advantage of not being one of the inner circles of servants at the house at the time of Marie's arrival. Marie liked the idea of having someone brought in from the outside even newer than Marie was. Of course, Jannette's connections with her mother would give that girl access to certain avenues of information not otherwise available to Marie. After all, it was very important for the mistress of any house to know the undercurrents at play in the servants' quarters if she ever hoped to keep a well-run establishment.

CHAPTER FOUR
SHADOWS DANCING

They made love in an isolated spot right out of some travel poster, complete with waterfall, vibrant exotic blossoms, and black-and-gray granite, among tropical greenery.

There was a pool at the base of the falls (the same falls Marie had seen the previous day from the vantage point that overlooked the estate on the way in from town). The water was deep and clear, its depths cluttered with massive car-size boulders that looked like giant billiard balls.

The spray supplied an occasional delicate mist that cooled the area pleasantly. Open to the sun, their picnic spot, surrounded by trees, was a beautiful interplay of color, light, and shadow.

They swam the water and made love again, Marie deciding the lead-in had been well worth it. Charles' lovemaking had definitely improved within such exotic surroundings. He was more spontaneous, more aggressive, and more physical than he'd ever been in London.

If Marie had had any doubts about this being Charles (had she actually imaged there being an identical twin out to play games with her?), she knew this body belonged exclusively to her man, right down to the small scar on its left shoulder, gotten as a result of a fall on a wooden garden stake when Charles was ten.

For the first time since her arrival, Marie actually was confident that things were going to be all right. If she'd had doubts, well those had been only because it was possibly just natural to question the motives which had rushed her into a hasty courtship, quick marriage, and sudden uprooting from the only life she'd ever known.

Love, of course, had been the scapegoat she'd used for every step along the way. Love for this handsomely exciting man who had suddenly appeared in her life at an otherwise thoroughly boring London party.

"I'll bet I can tell you more about the man you're planning to marry than even you know," Carolyne Nelson had told her daughter upon being informed Charles had proposed, "and I know very little, indeed, except he chooses to live on some isolated island in the Caribbean, even though he has money enough to live anywhere. He raises cacao, coffee, and little black Sambos. He's connected to the Blaines by some marriage of the Duke of Geoose to a lady-in-waiting of Empress Josephine during the days of the Napoleonic Court."

"I love him," Marie had insisted.

Certainly, she had loved the envious glances she'd gotten from friends, like Mildred Galen-Wayde. Certainly, she had loved the way Charles' stand-out tan made Englishmen pasty-complexioned in comparison. Certainly, she had loved the idea, too, of being whisked away from stuffy London society to a place in the sun where primitive natives frolicked in half-naked idyllic bliss.

On the journey to Saint-Georges, having realized there had been those extenuating factors in attendance, Marie had wondered if she hadn't moved too quickly. However, now, once again, in Charles' strong arms, she regained her assurance that her love for this man had been the prime motivating force in her having picked him—not someone else—to be her husband.

The two returned to the water of the pool, splashing and enjoying themselves like youngsters feeling deliciously wicked in indulging, once again, in co-educational nudity.

It was Marie who was first back out of the water. She came up on a flat stone that was toasted warm in the sun. Using the flats of her hands, she scraped drops of liquid off her tanning flesh, watching Charles still swim the cool water.

He moved gracefully. His body, slightly distorted by the liquid around and over it, sliced through the liquid like some exquisite machine or animal designed just for aquatic exploration. When he reached the far side, he turned in the water, using his feet to kick off the far shore, much like Marie had so often seen Olympic swimmers do. The pool swirled behind him, forming myriad vortexes and eddies that caught the sunlight and refracted it into shards of brilliance.

Marie experienced a decidedly warm and erotic sensation from just watching her husband's movements. Eroticism of this particular metal hadn't been at all a part of their courtship or their marriage in London.

Having seen what she had of the island, so far, Marie thought she might have a hint as to what kept Charles anchored to this particular stretch of ground instead of to any of the major world capitals. Saint-Georges was beautiful beyond belief. It offered everything he needed for a comfortable existence. It allowed him the exercise and outdoor living which would keep him physically fit while his counterparts in the big cities grew fat. While there was undoubtedly an island class system (Charles had briefly mentioned the need to introduce Marie to Saint-Georges' society), it would— Marie suspected—be far more to the tastes of a relaxed and informal man than the more rigid structure found in either London, Paris, or New York.

Yes, drying off in the warmth of a tropical sun, turning another shade of heavenly bronze that would have had her mother clucking her tongue and issuing warnings about skin cancer, Marie was more than happy to have snatched the opportunity to come here with Charles. She was becoming more and more sure that her paranoia of the past few hours could be attributed solely to her sickness on the ship, her exhaustion from too much travel all at once, the trauma of trying to settle into a strange place, and her initial apprehension that she might have acted rashly in the first place.

She reached for the tablecloth which Karena had

packed in the picnic hamper. Coming to her feet, she draped the pale blue cotton around her body like a native sarong. Doing so made her feel even more like a real islander.

She was headed around the shore toward the spot where she thought Charles would touch upon his next return from the far side of the pool when something caught her attention out of the corner of one eye. At first, she thought it was a small bird, then possibly a berry, fruit, or even a nut. Then she saw that, whatever it as, it was hanging from the branch of a large bush just off to one side of where she was walking. She detoured for a closer look.

It was a small figurine, carved from some kind of black wood, and threaded with a leather thong through a hole in its head. The leather, knotted by its two ends formed the loop from which the wooden pendant hung.

On first appearance, Marie suspected that the branch had inadvertently snagged the prize of some unsuspecting passerby who had continued on without it. However, closer inspection proved the thong so placed within the branch that it couldn't have possibly gotten there by mistake. To get it free, Marie first had to untie the knot completely. That meant that someone had specifically placed it there, probably some swimmer who hadn't wanted to lose it. Yet, if such precautions had been initially taken, why had the necklace been forgotten?

The figurine untied, Marie brought it up for a closer look. Certainly, it was an ugly little carving. It had bulged eyeballs, arched brows, roughly carved holes for nostrils, and a gaping mouth that came complete with obscenely parted lips.

"What do you have there?" Charles asked from behind his wife, giving Marie a decided start.

"Oh, Charles, you scared me," she said, punctuating with a nervous laugh of relief. Her right hand, holding to the little wooden pendant, had gone to her throat. Suddenly, she realized he wasn't looking at her but at the talisman.

He got that same glassy expression on his face that he'd had that morning over breakfast. In one quick second, Marie felt all of her previous contentment drain to the ground beneath her feet.

"Cécile, you're going to be the ruin of both of us, yet; you know that, don't you?" Charles said. His body was glossed with water from the pool. The veneer of slick liquid reflected sunlight to blind Marie as he took the few remaining steps that separated him from her.

"Charles?" she asked uncertainly. She didn't know what else to do or say. His eyes, once focused on the wooden figurine, now seemed focused on nothing in particular. His large blue pupils were strangely dilated for the amount of sunlight having access to them. "Charles?"

She thought he reached for the necklace; she moved to hand it to him, but his hands settled gently on her neck, instead.

She experienced a shiver and chided herself for whatever the fear suddenly having taken root inside of her.

"Why? Why?" Charles asked. His face looked decidedly pained; lines formed at the corners of his eyes and mouth where they hadn't been before.

"Why *what,* Charles?" Marie asked. She couldn't think of anything else to say. Yet, what she had said seemed highly inadequate for the occasion.

"I love you," he said.

Marie continued to have the impression he wasn't presently talking to her. To whom, then? Had he called her...Cécile?

"I love you, too, Charles," she said, wondering when he was going to come out of his trancelike state, this time around. At the breakfast table, it had been gone in mere seconds.

"Anyway, I think I love you," he said. "Sometimes I get confused. Sometimes I can't help but wonder. You know what they're saying, don't you?"

"No, Charles. What are they saying?"

"They're saying you're a witch who has seduced me; broken all of the rules because of your lust; condemned us, and all around us, to destruction."

Marie had yet another shiver. Bumps, like large icy beads, arose along her flesh. She tried to say something, even got her mouth open to do so, only to realize that Charles' hands gradually tightened around her neck.

"Are you a witch, Cécile?" he asked, his hands clamping event tighter into the softness of his wife's pretty throat. "Are the two of us really working together to conjure a hell upon this earth?"

"Charles, you're hurting me." Marie was plunged into some horrific nightmare. How could she possibly have gone from ecstatic bliss to this new low in such a few short minutes?

She dropped the wooden pendant and brought both of her hands to her neck to parenthesize his. She tried to relieve some of his squeezing pressure. Then, she tried even harder to get free, finding it more and more difficult to breathe. Definitely, she had let things come too far. Yet, how was she to have known Charles was planning to choke her? He was her husband. He loved her. She loved him.

He...couldn't...be...doing...this!

"Charles!" Marie thought she was the one to voice that exclamation which made her husband suddenly turn loose.

She dropped to her knees on the ground, gasping for air. She had been on the verge of passing out. She knew it. She wasn't sure, even now, she wasn't losing consciousness. Everything was swimming in front of her eyes.

What seemed like long minutes of struggling to regain perspective must, in reality, have been only mere seconds, because, when Marie finally focused again, Charles was still standing pretty much in the same place. He had turned slightly to look at the old woman and the two men who stood just a few feet away within the shadows of the thick underbrush.

"Charles!" the old woman snapped.

For the first time, Marie realized it had been the

woman's previous command, not anything said by Marie, which had caused Charles to free his stranglehold.

Charles clamped a hand to each temple, as if struck by a sharp pain to his brain. By way of enforcing that illusion, he let out a low, animalistic groan that sent new rills of terror coursing through Marie's veins.

His arms dropped limply to his sides. He turned ever so slightly, and Marie felt he was actually, finally, seeing her again.

"Marie?" he asked in verification. His voice was low, almost a whisper.

He collapsed, his head audibly striking a rock as he slumped to a heap on the ground.

* * * * * * *

Marie paced her bedroom, furious. More than that, she was sick with worry. Not only had Charles had some sort of attack at the pool, to which Marie still couldn't put rhyme or reason, but his head had received a nasty bump when he fell.

The old woman and the two natives had taken firm charge of the situation, acting much as if Marie wasn't even there. They had loaded Charles on his horse, much as if he were a sack of potatoes, and had brought him back to the house—Marie following after. Admittedly, Marie, by that point, had been a bit hysterical. She had cried and was still crying, her face streaked with tears. Her eyes were red. Her nose was runny. Her cheeks were unattractively puffy.

She would see her husband! They couldn't continue to keep her from him. She didn't care what they said or did; she was mistress of his house. She was Charles Camaux's wife. She had more right to be at her husband's bedside than that old woman and the old hag's two native cohorts. If that trio persisted in keeping her out, each and every one of them would pay dearly if—no, not *if*, but *when*—Charles came out of his coma and got back on his feet.

She went to the mirror over her vanity table. Her reflection verified what she already knew: she looked a sight! There was no reason why she should have expected to look anything but...after what had happened.

She headed into the sitting room, and, then, to the door leading to the hallway. She took three deep breaths and opened the door. She came out, turned a sharp left and started toward her husband's suite.

The two men who had been with the old woman at the pool were stationed outside Charles' door, much like a pair of half-naked palace guards.

Marie put on an expression that dared either of them to challenge her right to do what she was doing. If they tried to interfere, she would bring down the house with her screams. These savages hadn't seen anything until they got a good look at a girl of good English stock once her feathers were really ruffled.

Neither man made any attempt whatsoever to stop her. They just stood there, much like wooden dummies, their muscled arms folded over their muscled chests.

She shut the door behind her, only sorry for the loud bang she made in slamming it if just because her husband, after all, had a head injury that likely wasn't helped by Marie's burst of childish chagrin.

She was going to have to stop acting like a school-girl and more like mistress of the house if she wanted to be treated like the latter. In a way, she could even admit—albeit reluctantly—that it was a good thing the old woman and the men had been there at the pool to take charge when Charles had collapsed. Marie couldn't have gotten her husband back to the house on her own.

On the other hand, it was possibly the old lady's shouts which made Charles collapse in the first place. Marie refused to believe her husband would have continued to strangle her. More likely, he would have come to his senses, shortly, with none of his collapsing and bumping his head.

How long, anyway, had those three been there, watching and spying? Long enough to have seen all that had come before? Even the thought of any of them having seen her swimming naked, or....Her already tear-pink cheeks reddened even more.

She would fire that old woman from the staff! She wouldn't stand that creature forever lurking in the shadows like the ghoul she was, spying on the intimate moments between a man and his wife.

Charles' rooms were dark. Marie pushed away from the door as soon as her eyes made out the gauntlet of furniture she needed to maneuver to get to the adjoining room that held her husband in his bed.

He wasn't conscious when she reached him. Thank heaven, though, he obviously wasn't dead, either. He breathed evenly, more as if asleep than anything. A corner of his forehead showed discoloration even in the shadows.

Marie sat on the edge of his bed. She reached out her hand and gently touched his face. His skin was cool which, along with the tempo of his breathing, were definitely good signs.

She gave a quick, darting glance around the room, somewhat surprised she was really alone with her husband. Genuinely, she expected to see the old woman somewhere within the shadows, watching to make sure Marie didn't cause any fuss.

That was another thing that got Marie worked up: the unavoidable feeling that the old woman blamed Marie for everything that had happened, when it was Charles, not Marie, who was showing a side never exhibited in London. Supposedly, Marie had married a rather prim and proper man in England, who had metamorphosed into something quite different on Saint-Georges. Not that Marie was complaining about all of the changes; but, when one purchased the salt of the earth, one expected to find salt, not something else.

Undoubtedly, Carolyne Nelson would have been surprised by some of the change in her son-in-law.

"Just a little bit stuffy for someone as well off and as good looking as he is, wouldn't you say?" Carolyne had asked on the eve of her daughter's wedding. Although, it wasn't the first or the last of her hints that her daughter should think twice before attaching herself to Charles Camaux. Not that Carolyne managed to come up with anything factually derogatory, although she might well have sent someone off to Saint-Georges to snoop if the couple had only allowed her sufficient time. Marie thought, now, that maybe her mother had had a way of intuitively sensing things that "weren't quite right". However, even Carolyne would have to admit her intuition hadn't saved her from her three disastrous marriages, going on four; her latest problems, resulted from a spouse twenty years her junior, and had left her much too occupied, and much too exhausted, to give as much time as she might normally have devoted to delving into her daughter's hasty courtship.

Charles stirred in his sleep (unconscious?), and he mumbled something briefly and completely undecipherable.

Marie sat back to stare at his face. His features were handsome, even in a relaxed state, like now. He had such long eyelashes. She hadn't ever really noticed before just how long they were.

"What is happening, Charles?" she whispered, resting the flat of her hand along the left side of his face. "Who is Cécile? Who is that old woman? What are these spells you're having? Would you really have kept on strangling me if the old hag hadn't showed up to stop you? How can I possibly help you, if you continue to leave me in the dark?"

She sensed, rather than heard, activity in the downstairs of the house. Conditions had apparently heightened her intuitive senses.

She left the bedroom, passed through the outer room, and came back into the hallway. She paid no attention to the men still at the door. In turn, they paid no seeming attention to her.

She walked to the balustrade and looked down into the area below, seeing nothing. She heard nothing, either. Yet, she continued to *sense* something.

She went down the stairs and surprised Madeleine who was exiting the den. The colored girl looked wide-eyed, as if she wanted to run somewhere but didn't know where, or even have a clue as to how to begin.

"Do we have a visitor, Madeleine?" Marie asked, trying to pretend as if she felt absolutely nothing out of the ordinary. Madeleine, though, wasn't able to follow Marie's cue. She looked terrified. She acted terrified. She continued to appear as if the very sight of Marie struck her quite deaf and dumb.

Marie saw the girl's nervous glances back toward the den and decided to take Madeleine out of her obvious misery by moving on. She headed for the den, and Madeleine disappeared up the stairs at a run. Marie pulled open the sliding doors that gave access to the book-lined enclave.

At first, she mistook the room as empty. However, that misconception was soon alleviated by a shattering of glass.

She saw the man struggling to rescue a crystal decanter, tipped over on a corner table, and bubbling cognac across a highly waxed tabletop. The decanter had broken a snifter when falling, shiny shards of the latter like minor icebergs amid a gushing sea of spilling amber liquid.

"Father?" Marie asked; obviously, the man was a priest.

He had long, matted grey head hair, echoed by a long and matted grey beard. His reversed collar was anything but clean. His dark suit was neither clean nor pressed. His hands shook as he tried, once again, to pour himself another drink, paying little attention to the mess already made.

Finally bringing a full glass of brandy to his pouty lips and drinking, he eyed Marie over the edge of his snifter, like a child caught having pilfered from a cookie jar.

"Who are you?" he asked when he finally stopped drinking. He'd diminished his glass of booze by half.

"I already know who *I* am, thank you," Marie replied. She'd had about enough of people bossing her around, and here looked someone she might very well handle. "The more pertinent question seems to be: Who are *you?*"

He didn't seem impressed. Then, he was already in somewhat of a drunken stupor. He'd been drinking long before he worked up the guts to come here to learn if the rumors were true. He took another swallow, finishing off what was left in his glass. When he spoke, his words were more than a little slurred.

"Who am I?" He greedily eyed the now upright

and partially filled decanter. "Who am I? Where do you come from that you don't know Father Carl Westbrook?"

Definitely, Marie wasn't impressed. As far as she was concerned, Father Carl Westbrook was obviously a priest on the slide—if he was a priest at all.

"Well, Father Carl Westbrook...." She paused to inject: "Please, do have another drink." She watched as he proceeded to do just that. He was no steadier pouring this time than last. "No matter what they might have told you, Father, I hardly think my husband is yet ready for a priest. I would have thought everyone's time put to far better use had they summoned a doctor."

Westbrook's latest glass of booze stopped at his lips.

"Your husband?" He tried to get Marie into focus.

"You're in *my* house, Father Westbrook. Charles Camaux is my husband. He's had an accident. I thought that was why you were here. He's...."

"He's a fool!" Westbrook said loudly. He'd not yet sampled anything from his latest glassful. "Your husband...Madame...is...a...certifiable...fool!"

He gulped the cognac in one massive swallow that made his large Adam's apple bob beneath his collar.

"You tell him that for me, Mrs. Camaux. You tell him Father Westbrook—oh, yes, he'll remember me—said that's what he is, too!"

He smacked his empty glass down on the tabletop with a force so great that Marie marveled any of the crystal withstood the shock.

Staggering, he left the room.

Marie let him go. She doubted he was sober enough to give her any real answers, so she left him to be one more mystery in a series of building mysteries to which she was determined, eventually, to have answers.

He exited through the large front doors of the house, letting them close with a loud, shuttering rumble behind him. Marie felt the resulting vibrations ominously pass through the floor beneath her feet.

* * * * * * *

It wasn't yet daylight. For not the first time, that was something Marie sensed before opening her eyes. When she did open them, blackness was silhouetted within the window. The curtains remained opened from the day before. No servant had bothered to close them. Madeleine had been the only household servant Marie had seen during the course of the whole previous evening: emerging from the den to the stairs, then, briefly, when the young girl had silently delivered a platter of cold meats, salad, and white wine from Karena (the dirty dishes still on a small table in Marie's sitting room). Marie didn't consider the two taciturn men, who'd remained on Charles' door, as official members of the household, having never seen them before their appearance at the pool; she still hadn't the faintest notion who they were or from where they'd come.

She rearranged her bed clothes and tried to find a more comfortable position, all with little success. She was surprised she'd been able to sleep at all. That she had dozed was the best indication of just how thoroughly drained, physically and mentally, she had become.

She shut her eyes, telling herself that, come morning, she was determined to get to the bottom of "things". Surely, there was someone who had the answers besides the mute cabal in the house and on the estate grounds. Who? What made Marie think they would talk to her?

She refused to go on the way she was. She wouldn't leave Charles while he was possibly in danger from concussion, or other complications, from his fall, but, after those crises were over, she could make no guarantees she was going to stay. Granted, she had promised to stick with Charles for better, or for worse, but there was a limit. The advantages Marie had known in marrying Charles came very close to being completely overridden by the disadvantages. Whether it was apparent to anyone else, or not, Marie was well aware her husband needed help that went beyond his recently bumped head. Why hadn't a medical doctor been summoned? Why hadn't Marie insisted upon one? What made her so thoroughly accept the authority wielded by that old woman?

Who had sent for Father Westbrook? Had someone suspected Charles' problem was more spiritual than anything else? Or had the "good" Father simply picked that particular moment to make a courtesy call on Charles Camaux and his new bride? The latter hardly seemed likely. There had been nothing courteous about

Father Westbrook. He had seemed genuinely surprised to find a Mrs. Camaux on the premises.

Marie realized sleep was presently quite out of the question. So was doing something to pass the time, until morning, like reading a book. She was incapable of concentrating on anything except her disarrayed state of affairs. Such thoughts were doubly frustrating, since Marie couldn't be all that sure just what her status was. She was Marie Camaux; she knew that much. She was the wife of Charles Camaux. Yet, there was an old woman wandering around who was obviously more in charge of things than the mistress of the manor.

Not that Marie could say any of the servants had been downright disrespectful. Even the two men outside Charles' door hadn't done anything genuinely offensive; they'd let Marie by when she had finally gotten up the spirit necessary to make the attempt. Before that, the old woman had merely told her to go to her room; Marie—assuming there was no way to fight her way through the human barriers—had done as she had been told. In retrospect, she could wonder if the two men had ever been as threatening as she'd originally imagined. Oh, they looked mean. How could they help but not, both six feet tall, well-muscled, and with seemingly perpetual sneers? In the final analysis, though, the only man to have physically manhandled her had been her own husband. As far as she could determine, he had, by doing so, come the closest to doing her bodily harm.

Far from being purposely disrespectful, Madeleine

had seemed more like a frightened animal. The rest of the staff had somehow managed to fade into the woodwork, although they obviously had remained cognizant of the prevailing circumstances; since, Karena had managed to prepare something for Marie to eat in her room, once it became obvious the mistress wouldn't be coming down to dine.

While Marie recognized that the quickest solution to everything was simply to have Charles regain consciousness and explain it all, that didn't relieve her confusion at the moment.

She opened her eyes, again, this time to fluff her pillow beneath her head. It was, then, she noticed the shadows in movement.

She watched, fascinated and frightened, as dark merged with light to cause a swirling effect on a large section of the ceiling and walls. For several long seconds, she was completely unable to reason the cause: it looked like the very same mixture of shadow and light often seen at the bottom of shallow pools.

Before she reached the conclusion that her nervous condition had brought her to the point of hallucinating, she realized what she saw was the result of something occurring outside and distorted by the window.

She threw back the blankets and got out of bed, realizing that what she saw was a replay of those kinds of shadows that danced across the walls and ceilings in darkened room whenever firelight was in play.

Was the house on fire? That thought was exceptionally terrifying to a woman whose husband was unconscious just down the hall. How would she get Charles out of the burning Château if the servants, as well as the two muscled men panicked, too busy trying to save themselves to be concerned about their master? There was no way Marie could lug Charles down the stairs and out the front door without help. While Charles' muscled body gave him exceptional strength when he was conscious, that same muscle, when he was in a coma, was dead weight that Marie would be hard-pressed to drag even a few feet, let alone the full distance.

However, if it was a fire, Marie was apparently the only one aware of it. Even as she was up and across the carpet to the window, the house remained quiet.

What she discovered, upon looking outside, took her breath away. If she had correctly analyzed the reflections as having been flame-caused, it was hardly what she expected.

Out there, weaving, like a slow-moving serpent, was a long line of figures carrying lighted torches. The flickering flames had the night battling to reclaim its supremacy. Shadows and light fought for control, converting the whole backyard into a maze of shifting designs through which moved—how many?—people. There had to be at least a hundred. Going where?

Marie turned from the window and reached for her robe on a nearby chair, tripping on a footstool as she did so. She hardly noticed the pain of her bruised shin, so anxious was she to put definition to this latest night-time madness.

Any initial fears that the house was being set to torch by natives was put to rest. The figures weren't moving toward the house but away from it. The torch-bearers weren't running helter-skelter, or jumping up and down: stereotypical actions of savages run amok.

Actually, Marie had a firm inclination to stay right where she was. The idea of one lone woman rushing out to confront a hundred figures with torches had not a little bit of madness to it. She was driven, though, by an inner knowledge that too many unsolved mysteries were liable to make her crack under the strain. Somehow, somewhere, there had to be some speck of reason to the general overall confusion. She was determined to get one piece of it, this piece of it, before this latest macabre happening became but one more inexplicable cipher.

She reached the door to the hallway and slowly opened it a crack to look out. The house was dark, but her eyes adjusted well enough to distinguish solid objects from ethereal shadow.

Convinced the coast was clear, she stepped out, leaving her door ajar, just in case she was forced to make a sudden retreat back through it.

She headed for the stairs, aborting only when she realized her husband's door was absent its two human sentries.

She went into her husband's suite.

Its outer room had its walls and ceiling splattered with the same shifting shadows Marie had left behind her, since his rooms, too, looked out on the same stretch of back lawn as hers, through which the torchbearers still marched.

In her husband's bedroom, though, it wasn't the play of shadow which caught her attention.

His bed was empty!

"Charles?" She thought he must have gotten up for some reason.

If he was up, he apparently wasn't scheduled for any quick return, if just because his bed was made, as if he'd never laid comatose in it.

"Charles?" Marie called again, this time louder. Her voice was somehow swallowed by the room.

She was on the verge of tears. Only pure willpower kept her from them. She told herself, over and over, that converting to a weeping female wasn't going to solve any of her problems, or answer any of her questions. She was merely upset by certain things that distorted. Obviously, there was even a logical reason for what was happening, then and there, just as there were logical reasons for everything that had come before. She shouldn't get so worked up until all of the facts were in for proper analysis.

Still, *telling* herself to be calm, cool, and collected, was not the same as *being* calm, cool, and collected.

If she thought there could be more gained by hiding in some dark corner, waiting for startling revelations miraculously to appear, then she would have gone to that corner straightaway. Somehow, though, she suspected any answers as to what was happening would have to be gleaned, then and there, or probably not at all.

She proceeded from her husband's room to the stairs. She stumbled twice, once almost having a serious fall. Both times, she recovered.

She crossed the downstairs rooms in the dark, heading for the French doors that opened out onto the veranda that overlooked the back lawn. It took all of her effort to keep her feet moving, one in front of the other. Her brain kept insisting she stop.

What was this madness she was forcing herself to meet head on? What could she possibly hope to gain: one woman against a hundred people with torches? How could she believe there would be anyone to answer her questions, there, amidst those macabre circumstances?

She unlatched the French doors and threw them open. She stepped out onto the veranda, her face and body instantly a screen for the flickering torchlight in the darkness.

Before and below her, there was a seemingly endless line of figures, men and women, holding sticks topped with flame. The line stretched all of the way across the lawn and into the edge of the jungle.

She turned toward a sound off to her right, confronting a life-size version of the wooden figurine she'd found hanging from the bush at the pool. It was the very same grotesque and ugly creature with its bulging eyes, and its obscenely parted lips.

It came closer, towards her.

She did what she had only done a very few times in her twenty-six years. She fainted, somehow finding the blackness of the unknown far more preferable to an inexplicable reality she couldn't comprehend.

CHAPTER FIVE
BURNT OFFERING

Whatever she was dreaming (something about being chased by a big black man with a machete, both of them running through a forest of burning trees), Marie came awake with a start that shot her into a sitting position.

"Easy, darling, easy," Charles consoled. He was sitting on the edge of her bed. He proceeded to enfold her in a comforting embrace.

"Oh, Charles, it was horrible!" She buried her face against his chest. He smelled of lime-based after-shave or cologne.

"It was nothing but a nightmare, honey," he assured her. "It's all over now."

She gave a grateful shudder and pulled reluctantly away from the protectiveness of his strong body. A good look at her husband's forehead, with its bump and discolored bruise, told her that one nightmare might be over, but a more horrible one was possibly about to resume where it had left off the night before.

"You had me worried sick!" she exclaimed.

"Me? I'm fine." He flashed a wide smile that set off his dimples to their best advantage. "Except for a slight headache."

"You'll have to see a doctor," she said. "That could still turn out to be something really serious."

"Let's see how it is in a couple of days? If it's not completely healed by then, I'll go see a doctor. Okay? Okay!"

Marie had to admit that he didn't seem any the worse for wear. Certainly, he seemed, once again, to be completely rational.

"I hear you had quite a scare last night," he changed the subject. "I should apologize for not being around to explain it all to you. I'm afraid none of the servants felt comfortable enough to make explanations, which caused you more concern than you need have had."

"You mean there's an explanation for the scene I saw on our lawn last night?"

"You can well imagine the talking down I gave Lucie when I heard she and her cohorts had you collapsing on our veranda," Charles said. "I assure you, they won't be doing it again soon. Such ceremonies are few and far between. However, next time you wake up to find a procession of islanders bearing torches across our yard, you'll know a little more about it, won't you."

"Will I?" Marie countered. "If so, you're going to have to be a lot freer with your information, because, right now, I know no more about what happened last night than I did last night when confronted by...by...by...whatever that 'thing' was that appeared out of the darkness on our veranda."

Assured that he was all right, Marie was determined

not to let him out of her sight until he gave her some logical explanations. She had no desire to go through another night like the one just endured.

"That thing, as you put it, was really a 'she'," Charles said. "Or, rather it was one of the village women made up to look like Fyrea."

"Fyrea?"

"Probably a bastardization of the French word for fire. The older natives, I hear, have a name for Her that goes back before the French arrived on Saint-Georges, but I've never heard it. I suppose every deity must have its own special name to be used only in sacred ritual, away from hearing infidel ears."

"I'm afraid I don't understand. You mean that ceremony, last night, had some kind of religious significance?"

"That surprises you?"

"I suppose it does. I assumed the islanders were all Christian."

"Oh, but there certainly are many of those." Charles gave his wife a surely-none-of-this-is-really-all-that-strange look; for Marie, though, it *was* strange. "They've accepted Christ, but they've not surrendered their old gods, either. They rather like to hedge their bets, if you know what I mean."

"While on the subject of religion...." Marie was tempted to interject a reference to Father Westbrook's visit, but she thought there was no sense in moving on to an entirely new subject until this one had been discussed more thoroughly. "What exactly were they doing last night?"

"They're convinced The Cauldron is going to erupt any day now and swallow us all up in fire and brimstone." He must have been amused by the resulting expression on Marie's face, because he gave another of his thoroughly captivating and good-humored laughs. "Don't worry your pretty little head, though, my dear. Every ten years or so, the rumor goes around that The Cauldron is about to start bubbling again. The natives revert temporarily to the primitive, quite content to believe, in the end, that their incantations and little dances save the day. It's all rather harmless if taken in proper context."

"You were out there with them?" She couldn't forget her panic when she'd gone to his bedroom and found him gone.

"Purely as an observer, in my capacity as major landowner hereabouts." He sounded genuinely sorry for how things had turned out. "The natives need a white authority figure on hand to give them that little extra incentive to keep things in check. I apologize profusely for not telling you I was going. Lucie said you were in your room asleep. I'm afraid I figured, what with everything else you had gone through yesterday, that you would probably sleep through the whole silly thing. While I'm apologizing, by the way, let me add my regrets about what happened at the pool. I'm afraid I haven't the foggiest notion what got into me, unless it was just too much heat during our morning ride to get there. Rest assured that it certainly won't happen again. Did I hurt you?"

"I was a little shaken, that's all."

"Well," Charles said, and he gave an accompanying shrug, "the sun has been known to cause some people to do some mighty strange things. I have to admit that was the first time I've done anything quite so crazy, though."

Marie began to feel a little easier. Just as she expected, all she needed to clear up the muddied waters was a new day and her husband to provide rational explanations. The little ceremony was certainly feasible. The natives on Haiti somehow had managed to combine pagan and Christian doctrines into one mishmash religion. So, why not something similar on Saint-Georges? Too much sun, even for a man who was used to its tropical glare, could probably, on occasion, take its toll. If Marie insisted Charles wear a hat, she might be assured there would be no recurrences of his performance by the pool. However, she wasn't finished with her enlightenment yet.

"Who's Lucie?" she asked. Charles had already mentioned her twice in their conversation that morning.

"You know Lucie," he insisted. "Lucie Bruay. You met her your very first day."

Marie began a quick mental rundown on the staff, giving faces to all the available names: Petre, Karena, Madeleine, Marc, Julie, Rolphe....

"Come on, now, Marie," Charles chided, as if his wife had to be feigning ignorance.

Suddenly, it struck Marie as to whom Charles

referred. So, the old woman had a name. Lucie Bruay. Up until then, Marie hadn't even thought of putting a name to the gnarled old gnome. Names were for people. Marie hadn't brought herself to think of Lucie as anything more or less than a decidedly malignant force that had somehow, uninvited, entered Marie's life.

"I don't like her!" Even as she said it, she realized she was likely coming across like a pouty child. After all, what had Lucie *really* done to her? Whatever the hag's faults, they might easily be forgiven when taken as indications of the woman's approaching senility. If it hadn't been for Lucie on the scene by the pool, Charles might still have been lying there unconscious. Although, Marie was confident she would have managed—somehow—to get help on her own.

"She does take a little getting used to, I'll grant you that," Charles agreed. If he was upset about his wife's out-and-out statement of dislike, he didn't show or say it. "She hates change. Any kind of change. If she had her way, she would set the calendar back and get rid of us all—herself included."

"She was watching us out by the pool, Charles."

Surely you're not insinuating Lucie has become some kind of prurient voyeur at her advanced age?" In seeming answer to his own question, he gave a low chuckle that mocked that possibility as ludicrous.

Marie wondered how she was somehow managing to come across the heavy in the scenario.

"Actually, she said they were out gathering roots,"

Charles said, his voice indicating Marie must see how that explanation had to take precedence over the other. "She's kind of the local shaman—or, is it sha*wo*man? She's not bad at it, either. She treated this bump on my head, didn't she? Look at me today, up and jumping."

"Just what is her capacity around the house?" Marie decided she had best get the lines established while she had Charles handy to draw them.

"I'm afraid I don't understand," he said, as if sincerely puzzled by her question.

"I mean, as far as the servants and the house goes, who has the final say? Me or Lucie Bruay?"

"What a strange question," he decided. There seemed no doubt about his actually believing it was strange, either. "You're my wife, my dear. Lucie is...well...is just Lucie. She isn't even officially a member of this household. I'm wondering whoever, or whatever, gave you the impression it was otherwise."

Marie could have given examples, like the woman having been at the head of the reception line, but she had second thoughts about coming across sounding like sour grapes. She should have been more assertive from the get-go. Some people were very much like children in that they had to be shown who was boss from the start or else they'd walk right over you. Give them an inch, and they'd take a mile, every time.

Well, she had given her last inch. Everyone—Lucie Bruay included—had taken the very last mile he or she could hope to get from Marie Camaux.

Madeleine interrupted with breakfast. The girl

looked just as nervous as she usually did. Marie was going to take a good look at every person on the household staff, and, if they didn't stand up to her close scrutiny, she would have them replaced by people who did. This was officially her domain, now, signed, sealed, and delivered. It was her home for the rest of her natural life. She had no desire to share it with people who didn't know where the real authority was. They would learn, and learn fast, or they would be replaced by people who could learn far faster.

"I thought I'd take the morning off to join you for breakfast for a change," Charles said, removing silver lids from sterling chafing dishes. "I hope you don't mind."

In fact, breakfast with Charles turned out to be the perfect beginning to Marie's new day. The only slightly sour note—and it was short-lived—was when she mentioned Father Westbrook.

"Was here? Last night?" Charles oh-so-gently replaced his coffee cup on its delicate China saucer.

"Drunk, I do very much believe," Marie said. "He wanted me to be sure to tell you that you were 'a certifiable fool'."

"Yes, that does, indeed, sound like Father Westbrook. I'm afraid he's the local eccentric...priest. I wouldn't be surprised if he isn't defrocked before long. Quite frankly, I'm surprised he hasn't been already. He can't have much of a congregation remaining. Anyway, if he comes by the house again, give me a call. If I'm not around, have Marc show him the door. The man is something of a bore, and his usual drunkenness is not only a disgrace to him and to the church, but it's never pleasant to see."

Charles asked Marie to please pass the blueberry muffins, and they drifted into making plans for how they would soon ride up the mountain to see the lake cupped within The Cauldron.

* * * * * * *

Her resolve seemed to get results. At least, the servants appeared to become more respectful the moment each was called in and informed that changes were possibly in the offing. Marie wanted them all to be on notice. In a couple of weeks, she would definitely decide who would stay and who would go. The only one Marie went so far as to assure a continued position was the cook. Marie couldn't but appreciatively remember how Karena had seen Marie got fed while the rest of the staff went into hiding. Of course, Madeleine had been visible, too, but there was something about Madeleine's continual state of hyper nervousness that made Marie, in turn, nervous. In the end, Marie thought the girl might have to go.

Since Lucie Bruay wasn't officially part of the staff, Marie could hardly give the old woman walking papers. On their next encounter, though, she was determined to let Lucie know, in no uncertain terms, that the old woman wouldn't be welcome at the château if she continued her haughty, mainly confrontational, ways.

Marie interviewed Karena's daughter, Jannette,

for the position of personal maid. She took to the girl immediately, telling herself it had absolutely nothing to do with Marie being anxious to try her hand at hiring now that she had put into motion the mechanics for future firings.

At fifteen, Jannette was tall for her age. In fact, she was almost as tall as Marie who stood at five-foot-six in stocking feet. She had mocha-colored skin that was clear and smooth. She had dark black eyes, and a black skullcap of kinky, close-cropped hair. She spoke pleasantly sing-song English. Though she spoke only when spoken to, she didn't give the impression (like Madeline was forever doing) that she was fearful the ground would open up at any moment and swallow her.

Throughout the interview, Marie did notice how Jannette had a tendency to finger the wooden charm on its leather-thong around her neck. Marie recognized the figurine as a smaller version of the one Marie had found attached to the bush by the pool, and which had made its "human" appearance on the veranda on the night of the torch-light procession.

Marie was tempted to query Jannette about her religious views, but she decided against it. She remembered the old adage about religion and politics being verboten as subjects for polite conversation. It was undoubtedly best to let people do their own "thing", as strange as that "thing" might be.

However, it was the sighting of Jannette's necklace which caused Marie, shortly after lunch, to decide to go in search of the pendant she remembered having dropped by the water. She had a horse saddled at the stables and started off. So indelibly had events inked the route into her brain, she doubted she would ever forget it, even if never required to travel it again. Although the path led through thick strands of trees and tangled underbrush, Charles had assured there were no longer any dangerous animals remaining on the island to hide in them.

"A couple of fat boars are rumored still to exist on the other side of the mountain," Charles had said when Marie had first voiced concern about the possibility of wildlife within the dense underbrush. "Aside from those, though, there are only the birds. Snakes, I guess, never managed to survive the swim to get here."

When Marie reached the pool, it looked just the same. Any sinister aura it now possessed was present only because Marie's imagination worked overtime.

She spent a good thirty minutes searching for the dropped pendant without finding it. She had covered the area so thoroughly, she was sure she would have located it if was still there. So, someone must have picked it up within the last twenty-four hours. Not that there was anything suspect in that. After all, Marie had found it only after someone else had, whether inadvertently or not, discarded it.

She wasn't even sure why she was so disappointed that her search proved unsuccessful; unless, as she suspected, she had been out for a souvenir. It would have been something to pull out, one day, to show her children and grandchildren; so, everyone could have a good laugh about the night Marie was scared out of her wits by torch-carrying natives on her lawn (no mention likely ever made of Charles' seizure and his attempted strangulation of his new bride).

Accepting defeat, finally, and getting a little jittery (was she actually seeing Lucie Bruay and that old hag's two gladiators hidden behind every bush and tree?), she un-tethered her horse and decided to do a bit of additional exploration before heading home. There was nothing pressing back at the house. She had already gone over dinner plans with Karena, having decided it was time the cook showed skills beyond cold-meat plates, breakfasts, and the occasional picnic basket.

There were several trails from which to choose, and Marie ended up letting her horse decide, while Marie merely concentrated on staying oriented. The last thing she needed or wanted was to get lost.

Having never done that well in school botany and biology classes, she still amused herself by trying to identify various species of indigenous plant life.

If she wasn't mistaken, there were mahogany and cedar trees. There were several varieties of palms; she counted at least ten different kinds before she finally left off. She thought she saw acana, cottonwood, and possibly rosewood. Lemon, lime, fig, and orange trees were, of course, easiest to identify, probably because they had telltale flowers and/or fruit ripening, in one stage or another.

Flowers were too numerous to try and classify. They hung in vibrant swaths of color, or in isolated dots, or drops, or drools, from the branches and vines, on all sides: purple, white, and green orchids; purple-red bracts of bougainvillea; red, yellow, and creamy hibiscus; exotic passion flowers in which several colors often fought for dominance within one large and impressive bloom.

She reined in her horse, because of some picked flowers: a large pile of them in a small clearing just off the trail. Left to decay in the heat of the tropical sun, the rotting blooms emitted an odor of thick sweetness that assaulted her senses with an almost physical force. The smell recalled visions of Marie as a small girl, standing frightened to death in small water closet, a broken bottle of perfume spilled at her feet.

Her eyes caught movement within the bows of surrounding trees where literally hundreds of black wood Fyrea figurines hung from leather thongs.

* * * * * * *

Made ill at ease by having stumbled upon what might well be a site of some pagan religious significance (maybe even the spot at which culminated the previous evening's torchlight parade?), Marie was made more sensitive to the possibility of trouble the minute she dismounted, back at the stables, and handed her horse over to Theodore. Her intuition was bolstered by Charles' sweat-covered horse being cooled down off to one side by another of the grooms.

"My husband is back?" There was no reason why he shouldn't be home at that hour; but, there was no way he would have overheated his horse without good reason. Marie would have considered such thoughts pure paranoia, but, considering the things that had happened over the last couple of days....

Quickly, she headed for the house, after making neither heads nor tails of the mumbled reply Theodore had given her. She wondered if all the natives had taken to communicating via undecipherable grunts.

Charles met her at the doorway.

"Marie, I'm glad you're here." He took his wife's arm and guided her into the den, sliding the doors closed behind them.

So far, he seemed normal, if obviously concerned about something. Marie was determined to keep an eye out. If she had learned nothing else since her arrival at Château Camaux, it was to keep on guard—even with her own husband.

"Something happened?" Her question was obviously superfluous; what she should have asked was: "*What* happened?"

"It's Father Westbrook," Charles said. "Maybe you'd better sit down."

"Father Westbrook? What about him?"

"He was drunk when you saw him, yesterday: isn't that what you said?"

"Very drunk, I should have said if I didn't."

"He left here alone?"

"If he had anyone with him, I certainly didn't catch a glimpse."

Charles sighed, went to the same decanter Father

Westbrook had used the previous evening (the priest's mess since cleaned up), and poured himself a drink. He motioned with the decanter by way of asking Marie if she wanted to join him. She shook her head. She had enough trouble keeping focused without clouding her brain with alcohol.

Charles took his snifter and came around to the couch. He patted the cushion next to his.

"Come and sit down," he said.

Marie convinced herself that whatever he had to say, it had nothing to do with another of his strange attacks; he was too lucid.

"It's all rather macabre," he said, taking a sip from his glass.

"What happened?"

"Apparently, he passed out last night on top of a volcanic steam vent, as far as anyone can tell. There's also the decided possibility that his horse threw him."

"A volcanic steam vent?" Marie blanched noticeably. No denying the wretched vision Charles' description conjured, but she wanted him to put even more definition to the unbelievable horror.

"You'll find the vents all over this mountain," he said. "They start up in one place, disappear after awhile, move on to someplace else a week or so later. A couple of years ago, we had a cluster of them appear in the basement of the hardware store in the downtown Villeneuve. Actually, they're usually of more help than hindrance, by way of offering escape valves for any buildups of pressure beneath the ground. Without them, I suspect, all the native praying by torchlight and offering up of gifts to Fyrea wouldn't do an ounce of good."

"When did they find him?" Although Marie had found Father Westbrook obnoxious, she certainly wouldn't have wished him this kind of end.

"Early this afternoon. The horse he borrowed from Gil Mason was grazing close by. I was just out there. It wasn't very pleasant."

"I can well imagine." Marie felt decidedly queasy.

"I suspect the police will be here any minute."

"Here?"

There was a rap on the door of the den. Marc announced a police car had just pulled to a stop in the driveway outside.

CHAPTER SIX
AUSPICIOUS SIGNS

Considering the potential for a disastrous evening inherent within the discovery of Father Westbrook's body, and the arrival of the police car at Château Camaux, the exact opposite occurred.

The police, who Marie expected to be around all afternoon and late into the night, asking her questions about the Father's visit the night before, were only at the house for a few minutes before Charles drove off with them to the site of the father's demise.

"I'll only be a little while," he had promised, giving Marie an affectionate kiss in parting.

Marie, though, had seen enough movies to know that no one ever went away with the police for just "a little while."

She only regretted not having had Karena prepare cold plates for that evening. Too late to inform the cook, though, of any menu changes, Marie couldn't picture herself managing a sit down, alone, to eat *potage aux concombres, salade mimosa, quenelles de poissons,* and *pigeonneaux sur canapés.* She steeled herself to make the best of it.

As it turned out, Charles was back in plenty of time for the evening meal. If his lead-up to dining had been too grisly to inspire ravenous eating, he managed to do justice in savoring everything, especially the *fantaisie bourbonnaise* served warm with heavy cream and washed down with *Veuve Clicquot*.

Accompanying Marie to her suite, he asked, rather like an embarrassed suitor, whether he might come in for awhile. The two ended up making love in Marie's big, four-poster bed, after which Charles mumbled drowsily that it suddenly seemed one long walk to his rooms and wondered if Marie would mind if he spent the night right where he was.

"I've been wondering why we have separate bedrooms," she said, smoothing a stray lock of black hair from her husband's brow; his eyes were lost behind closed eyelids which rested long and exceptionally black lashes against his cheeks. "Maybe, we could do some rearranging, do you suppose?"

"I'd like that." His voice was thick with approaching sleep. He rolled toward her, slightly, and Marie felt the powerful length of his muscled body against her left side. He threw one of his well-muscle arms easily across the top of her breasts and left it there.

During the following moments, her husband sleeping in bed beside her, Marie experienced seeming perfection. She seemed to have suddenly discovered the epitome of what married life should always be. She was happy in her marriage. She was happy to have come to Saint-Georges. She was happy to have surmounted whatever difficulties to arrive at this particular moment.

Then, as probably should have been expected, it was all spoiled in a mere couple of seconds, leaving Marie empty and slightly ill.

In that, Charles mumbled something in his sleep, something which Marie had first mistaken for the same undecipherable gibberish everyone, at one time or another, mutters when reality is fled and the dreaming state begins. Then, though, he muttered it yet again, distinctly and unmistakably—the name of a woman... not *Marie*.

Cécile.

Marie tried to console herself with the realization that Charles had, at least, waited until he was asleep. Had he spoken the woman's name while conscious, perhaps even in a moment of passion, Marie doubted she would have ever forgiven him. She would have been more apt to forgive him, even then (he might well have been entering a nightmare for all she knew), but she suddenly remembered the last time he'd mentioned that same name. Funny, Marie had disregarded that initial mention, until now, when she had been so certain, at the time, she would never forget anything that happened that afternoon by the pool.

"Cécile, you are going to be the ruin of both of us, you know that, don't you?" Charles had said, just before stepping up to Marie and wrapping his large and powerful hands around her neck. Then, there had been something about Cécile, *"a witch who had*

broken all of the rules because of her lust to seduce him," condemning them all to destruction.

Marie searched her memories for all of it. Had she, the first time around, attributed his voicing of that woman's name to temporary madness, during Charles' seizure? Had she thought the specter of this woman, whom her husband had once mistaken for her, wouldn't come back one night, like it had, to haunt her?

"Are you a witch, Cécile?" Charles had asked. "Are the two of us working together to conjure a hell upon this earth?"

Now, he dreamed of this woman. His sudden groan of accompaniment proclaimed the definite possibility that his dreams weren't all that pleasant, but that was of very little consolation to Marie. For whatever the reason, another woman (dream phantom or not) was in bed with them. Marie resented the other woman being there. Marie resented Charles for having, again, made Marie aware.

She took Charles' arm and moved it out of contact with her body. When he made an automatic move to replace it, she slipped from the bed to avoid him. She reached for her robe and wrapped it around her, suddenly chilled.

She walked to the window, pushing aside the heavy drapes so she could see outside.

The grounds were empty: nothing like she saw the night before. No shadows were sent dancing by torch flames. No natives were marching in a serpentine to heap a mountain of flowers beside some forest trail, and to string amulets of the pagan goddess, Fyrea, from the branches of jungle trees.

As Marie watched, as if by seeming magic, a huge cloud ascended toward the sky from the trees. It was a mass of blackness, much like smoke, and Marie was drawn helplessly back, once again, to think of fire, as she had last night when she had come awake to see shadows cavorting on the walls.

This time it wasn't fire, not even from hundreds of torches. It wasn't even smoke she saw but....

Birds. Hundreds...thousands...of ibis, heron, guacharo, parrot, buzzard, grouse, quail, toucan....

Marie opened the window, and the sound of all those simultaneously beating wings was a low thunder riding the night air.

She stepped out on the balcony, watching, fascinated as the birds moved en masse, this way, that way, and, then, suddenly veered in a long swooping movement toward the right and out to sea, leaving behind an intense stillness that was almost palatable.

Marie wondered how many people had been awake to witness that marvelous exodus. The marvel of it had completely erased, for a moment, Marie's very reason for having been where she'd been to see it.

She brought her right hand to her forehead, turning her fingertips wet with her perspiration. Her negligee and robe were damp and sticking to her body, much like the flowing drapery clung to an exquisite Greek sculpture.

It was hot and getting hotter. It was heat without

even a hint of a breeze to relieve it and its accompanying high humidity.

So quiet! Marie's ears strained to catch even one faint whisper of something. When sounds finally commenced, they were made even more disturbing because of the total silence which had preceded them.

No mistaking the whinnying horses. If Marie hadn't known there weren't any wild animals on the island, she would have guessed a bear, or wildcat, had gotten into the stables.

Suddenly, the fact the birds had taken flight but seconds before took on decidedly ominous implication that Marie wasn't able to define, although something told her she had been given sufficient pieces of the puzzle if she could only correctly fit them into place. It was something vaguely remembered about how birds roosted in darkness but very seldom flew after nightfall.

She returned to a room whose blackness was even greater than the night outside. She walked to the bed and sat on the edge of it.

"Charles?" She put her hand on his bare shoulder and shook him. "Charles?"

At first, she thought he wouldn't hear her, or respond. Then, she thought she was probably silly even to wake him. Yet, something continued to insinuate that the horses still made a fuss, even though the fallen-back-into-place curtains succeeded in muffling their sounds.

Charles mumbled something, opened his eyes, and, seeing Marie, smiled up at her.

"Something's wrong with the horses, Charles." She felt a little ridiculous. Why should she wake him because of the horses? Weren't there people paid good money to take care of just such things that occurred, day or night, in the stables?

"Wrong?" he asked. Sleep hadn't yet left him. His mind hadn't yet cleared sufficiently to register what she'd said.

"They're making quite a fuss," Marie said. "I was just out on the balcony, and I could hear them."

"The horses?" Charles stretched for his wristwatch removed earlier and placed on the stand by the bed. "What time is it?"

"About two."

"In the morning?" Simultaneously, he verified on his watch. He came to a sitting position, buckling the leather watchband around his wrist.

"Then, there were the birds...," Marie began, and, then, stopped. She couldn't quite put rhyme, or reason, to why the sudden exodus of fowl seemed important.

"What about the birds?" Charles asked. If he had been asleep but minutes before, he was fully awake now.

"A flock of them, all kinds, airborne, after dark," Marie said.

Charles came up out of bed and made a grab for his pants.

"Get downstairs!" he said. "Now!"

Marie didn't understand; she sensed, though, the urgency in his voice, and she obeyed, soon headed for the door.

Charles caught up with her at the head of the stairs, taking her hand and leading her down. Marie stumbled during the headlong dash, but Charles was quickly there to keep her from falling.

Halfway down, Marie saw the large crystal chandelier in the foyer begin its swing.

Less than a second later, the whole house was obviously moving violently beneath, around, and above her.

* * * * * *

Marie had never been in an earthquake. Her instincts, though, told her she was in a building composed of several million tons of granite that could tumble down around, or on, her and on Charles, at any minute. Therefore, she saw the openness of the great outdoors as their best salvation. As a result, she struggled frantically to get free when Charles jerked her to a sudden stop inside the Château's open front doorway and tried to anchor her to the spot.

By that time, the distinct earth rumbling verged on deafening. The only audible counterpoints to that frightening sound were the shrill screams of the servants.

Julie, the parlor maid, was out on the lawn, squealing like a banshee and careening round in a mad dance, like a drunk, as she desperately tried to maintain some semblance of balance on ground that was bucking beneath her.

Marc was out there, too, falling, first, here, and, then,

there, obviously disoriented by what was happening under and around him.

Madeleine (poor, frightened girl) made her appearance, with a screech of pure, unadulterated terror, as Charles finally succeeded in collapsing Marie into a position up close and personal to the doorjamb.

"It's safer here!" he kept screaming in Marie's ear as his wife continued her attempts to follow the servants out onto the lawn.

If Marie didn't believe him, she soon did.

With a loud crack, like the rending of a very thick and brittle tree trunk, the ground began to split. It began in the distance and raced from the jungle toward the Château. As the leading point of the crack commenced an even faster marathon across the lawn, its tail opened wider, forming a virtual canyon to which there was no apparent bottom.

Marc paused in an obvious daze while the earth split like an overripe melon beside him. For just an instant, Marie thought the crack had opened directly beneath the butler. Then, seeing that it hadn't, she assumed Marc was miraculously saved. Only to witness the ground beneath him collapse sideways into the steadily widening slit.

Marie screamed to warn him, but he was already only too aware of his dire situation to need any reminding by her. He tried to escape, but he lost his footing. He tried to claw for some kind of support, but, each and everything of which he attempted to take hold simply was more content to join him in his slide.

Marie tried to go to him, but Charles held her where she was. In the end, what could she have accomplished? Had there been any chance to offer reliable succor, Charles would have gone. Even a novice, though, could tell there was no rescue for the butler unless Marc rescued himself.

The black man clung tenaciously to the very lip of the crack, his feet dangling into the abyss.

Then, within seconds, he fell, and the canyon that had opened wide from him, closed in on him, giving the final impression that neither it, nor Marc, ever existed.

The loud noise of the earth in flux stopped, leaving a silence filled with thick dust and the sounds of people still in panic.

* * * * * * *

When the quake was over, there was no way to recall the exact terror experienced while it had been in process. Marie had to remind herself that it had happened at all: so little had seemingly changed in its aftermath. The lawn was back to one, large, well-manicured rectangle of grass, no headstone even to suggest Marc Demerol, butler, was buried there.

The house stood as if it had long stood, no noticeable chinks or cracks in its façade. If, inside, dishes and glassware were shattered and cracked, even that evidence of the cataclysm would soon be cleared away.

Marie soon realized she probably could have remained safe and snug in her bed, without all of the muss, fuss, and bother of waking Charles and fleeing downstairs.

"I hate to leave you, darling," he told her, having ushered Marie into the den and given her a glass of sherry to calm her shattered nerves, "but I have to check on death and damage in the surrounding area. Can you handle things at this end?"

"Sure." Marie succeeded in providing a wan smile. "What's a small earthquake, right?"

It hadn't been a small earthquake, though. Despite the evident little damage done around the Château Camaux, Villeneuve suffered extensive destruction, and most of the island villages had been completely flattened. As the quake had occurred during the night, there had been many casualties from buildings collapsing on the sleeping people inside.

* * * * * * *

"There must be something more I can do to help," Marie said to her exhausted husband. Frankly, she was appalled by the stories he'd brought back, detailing the extent of the damage done elsewhere by the earthquake.

A new day had dawned; hot and murky because of the greenhouse-effect caused by so many particulates still the air from the quake; as if the island was one giant dust mop that had just been shook.

Charles was slumped into a wing-backed chair, a glass of Scotch in his right hand. Marie would have preferred to see him eat something, but she made no comment. What he'd seen put Father Westbrook's tragic death in the shadow, and Charles undoubtedly deserved the drink he was having.

"Help?" Charles echoed after a pause; it had taken a little time for what his wife had said to register on his tired brain.

Marie was hardly encouraged by the *wonderful-thought-but* look Charles gave her. Then, again, men in crises seemed to imagine they were the only ones capable of pulling everyone through.

"Come on, darling!" Marie said with a patronizing lilt to her voice. "You're no longer talking to that screaming woman you were trying to spirit off to safety. This is your wife who is really very much concerned about people who have fared less well than she has in this catastrophe. I can surely be counted upon to at least render some badly needed moral support until more substantial aid arrives wherever it's needed."

"Yes, I should imagine you could," Charles admitted, although he still seemed reluctant to expose his wife to the disaster overly evident beyond the Edenesque grounds of the Château. Still, as meek and as mild as Englishwomen could sometimes seem, they weren't known for shirking in a pinch. There were still tales told, in more than one English pub, about female heroism on the home front during several wars.

"Marie, maybe it would be better if...." He left off, as if he didn't know quite how he was going to put what he had to say.

"I promise not to faint dead away at the first sight

of blood and embarrass you, darling," she promised. "Really, I feel quite my usual self again."

"It's just that Lucie Bruay is rather unofficially in charge of the local native injuries. And well...."

"That's not a very complimentary attitude to take toward your wife," Marie said, trying not to be hurt, since he was obviously only thinking of saving her feelings. "I'm not so petty as to make my obvious dislike of that woman keep me from momentarily putting myself under her authority for the purposes of offering succor."

If Lucie Bruay, Marie thought (didn't say), wanted to put on a show of lording it over Charles Camaux's wife, then that was Lucie Bruay's pettiness in the face of her people's suffering.

If Marie, though, had even that passing thought of Lucie indignantly refusing Marie's offer of assistance, it was misdirected. While not exactly welcoming Marie with open arms, Lucie wasn't her usual haughty, disdainful self, either. She showed Marie just what she wanted her to do (in the beginning, it was only tearing bandages from linen), and she delivered her instructions in a voice that was surprisingly devoid of all emotion whatsoever.

In the days that followed, Marie gained a definite appreciation of Lucie Bruay she hadn't had before. While obviously not a doctor in the traditional European sense, the old woman had an excellent bedside manner that never failed to calm and comfort even the most brutalized of the earthquake victims. On occasion, before helicopters began air-lifting in official doctors and medical supplies from Villeneuve (conditions at the capital had made for a two-day delay), Lucie could often be seen emptying contents of one bag of herbs or another into a tin cup and instructing her patients to drink the resulting brews. Whether or not her dosages were pure placebo, or genuine medicines, they usually brought favorable results. Marie, initially lulled into believing the quake had been insignificant, with little accompanying damage, appreciated anything that relieved the multitude of suffering which turned out to be the reality.

Not that Marie came to "like" Lucie. Nor, she suspected, did Lucie come to like Marie. For some reason, the battle lines had been indelibly drawn in the sand between the two women. What existed between them, for the moment, was merely a truce destined to last only for as long as victims remained in need on the battlefield.

As Marie moved up and down the rows of injured, giving whatever comfort she could, when and where it was needed, she was surprised to see that virtually every native (man, woman, and child) wore an amulet of the goddess Fyrea around his or her neck. In many cases, the talisman was worn side by side with the Christian crucifix. Just as often as not, though, it hung alone. Usually the victim, as if to gain some kind of comfort from the inanimate object, had one or both hands clasped around it. Many died with their fists never coming free of the figurine.

It wasn't easy or pleasant work. On the other hand, Marie found it strangely therapeutic. Granted, there was little time to have Karena whip up any further epicurean meals, but, when Marie was tired to the core, it was surprising how delectable a simple peanut butter sandwich and cup of tepid water could be. If she wasn't able to see as much of her husband as she would have liked, or if he was too tired to do much of anything but sleep whenever they did manage to climb simultaneously into the same bed, well, that didn't mean they weren't drawn closer together by the moment, because of the moment. In fact, as the last of the clean-up operations were finally visible on the horizon, Marie felt closer and more intimately involved with Charles than ever.

The only fly in the ointment was how Marie, whenever she found herself with Charles sleeping contentedly beside her, became so helplessly keyed up waiting for him, again, to call out Cécile's name. That he didn't do it, didn't keep her from thinking it would happen at any moment. When and if it did, everything would somehow, again, become different between them— even though Marie knew she didn't want that to happen.

Many times, she almost asked her husband, outright, the question which would clearly eliminate the mystery, once and for all! After all, for all she really knew, Cécile was an old nanny, or a favorite aunt, or even a cat. Then, Marie's jealousy would have been ridiculous and for nothing. It was, though, the fearful premise that Cécile was neither nanny, nor aunt, nor cat, which kept the question unasked and forever stuck in Marie's craw. For, she really wasn't sure she wanted him to identify the real Cécile. There was decidedly something to ignorance being bliss. On the other hand, she didn't like the way her jealousy steadily ate away inside her, especially if there was no real reason for it to be there in the first place.

CHAPTER SEVEN
MIST UPON THE MOUNTAIN

"Rise and shine!" Charles coaxed, giving Marie a loud good-morning kiss. He followed up by getting out of bed and drawing the drapes with a rustle that revealed a sky filled with the dim twilight of pre-dawn. Although he hadn't yet officially vacated his suite to take up official residence in Marie's, he was sleeping over, more and more, in his wife's bedroom.

"Charles?" Marie's eyes were blurry from sleep. She struggled to a sitting position on the bed. "Is something wrong?"

So often, these days, she feared waking up to birds (now returned) once again gone from their nests... neighing horses once again stomping their sharp hooves to vibrate the stables.

"This is *the* day we've been promising ourselves, my love." He disappeared into the bathroom but left the door open so the two could talk while he shaved; an additional eroding of their previous separate sleeping arrangements.

"What day?" She checked her watch and groaned, albeit silently, when she saw the earliness of the morning hour. Had she slept through the more enlightening first part of his conversation?

"The day we go up the mountain," he defined, obviously in good spirit. "It's about time we did more than just talk about it, don't you think? I figure today is just as good as any."

"Shouldn't we have let Karena know last night, so she could have fixed up a basket?"

"I'll take along a hook, line, and sinker. Even if your husband turns out to be less than an ideal fisherman, we'll likely find something to eat. Not that Karena and your recent regimens of French meals don't see me in need of a complete fast to off some of the recent poundage I've gained around my waistline."

Marie lost the next part of what he said when he turned on sink water to wet down his beard for shaving.

"...and cook them in the thermal pool," his voice came back loudly as the water turned off.

Any reference to any thermal pool always had Marie reminded of how Father Westbrook met his particular end by being cooked atop one. Thinking of Father Westbrook immediately had her thinking of the earthquake. Thinking of the earthquake....

Deciding such thoughts were hardly conducive to an enjoyable day with her husband, she decided to cast them aside. After all, there was nothing to indicate the last earthquake was a harbinger of greater catastrophes to follow. In its aftermath, more than one person was quick to point out how it was probably best the quake *had* come. Like those deadly moving vents that spewed live steam from the mountainside, earthquakes meant dangerous pressure beneath the ground was dissipated, a bit at a time, instead of in one massive big *BANG!*

A couple of university scientists had flown in from France and spent a couple of days at the Château while conducting tests.

"We can't seem to pinpoint anything to indicate Mont d'Esnembuc is going to erupt," the one, without the beard, had said casually over dinner one evening. Karena had outdone herself for the occasion, as if to prove one earthquake hadn't affected her culinary skills. Dessert was *farce aux fraises cio-cio-san.*

"The natives seem quite convinced it's only a matter of hours," Marie had observed.

"Then, maybe, the natives know something we don't," the bearded one had said, taking another large bite of the cake roll filled with its fresh strawberries, almonds, and kumquats. Just the way he said it insinuated that he hoped he had put any of the superstitious local twaddle to rest. However, a little later on, over coffee and cognac, the same scientist as much as admitted that, despite all of the modern technology available, accurate predictions hadn't been made to predict the recent eruption of Mt. Etna on Sicily. This, Marie figured, gave the two scientists about as much credibility as local diviners.

She threw back her blankets and got out of bed, comforted as to how earthquakes over the years on Saint-Georges hadn't been followed by violent volcanic outbursts. The nearest thing had been the earthquake of 1901, followed by a small river of molten lava which had wiped out a village on the east shore. Luckily, the village inhabitants had been completely evacuated to Isla Charlotte in time, except for a few stray dogs.

"Ah, you're up, then?" Charles congratulated, sticking his head through the open bathroom doorway. "I thought for a moment you'd gone back to sleep on me."

"Mmmmm," she moaned, as if that suggestion was a mighty tempting one—which it was. She sat on the edge of the bed and began searching for her slippers with the tip of her right toe.

"If you promise not to crawl back under the blankets, I'll shower in my own room," he said. "If I stay here, I'm sure to ask you to join me, and...."

"I know...I know." Marie laughed with genuine amusement. "Then, we would never get up the mountain. Right?"

"Exactly," he readily agreed.

* * * * * * *

Marie didn't believe him. She looked one more time at his amused grin, took another look at the foot-long fish with its olivaceous green hue and knew her husband had to be pulling her leg.

"Really, it *is*," Charles insisted, crossing his right hand over his heart like he would have done had they been children.

"How can it possibly be a *gold*fish if it's *green*?" She remembered the aquarium once had by a maiden aunt,

Mandy, in Walsham. "How can it be a goldfish when it's as big as a horse?"

"Culturists induce and strengthen the artificial golden color of the aquarium variety by controlling the amount of minerals in the water. What you see here is a goldfish that has been allowed to return to its natural state."

"A foot-long greenfish?"

"It's so big, because it now has a larger environment in which to live and grow. What fish do you know would risk growing to this natural size in any fishbowl?"

"I suppose you'll next tell me how you've a whale-size guppy up the trail just a bit." Marie watched him prepare the fish for boiling in the pool that dangerously steamed like crazy not four feet from where they sat.

"Why would I tell you that?" He smiled so wide that his dimples were like bullet holes in his cheeks. "That guppy story sounds like a real fish tale if I ever heard one."

He lowered his recent catch into the bubbling water, using the same hook and line with which, just a few moments before, he'd caught the monster, in a small, clear, stream nearby.

"I suppose I shall have to believe you." Marie folded her arms around her bent legs and rested her chin on her knees. She watched her husband's activities, enjoying just the watching—as she always enjoyed just the watching. "Although, my mother shall think I'm definitely going a little fishy when and if I should ever write how you and I shared a goldfish, between us, for lunch."

"Does sound a little ludicrous when described in quite that way." He checked his watch to make sure the fish wouldn't overcook and float free of its skeleton. "However, I don't think your mother is the type to be all that interested in how my grandfather, an avid dabbler in amateur ichthyology, decided an island with so many fresh-water streams and ponds deserved some fresh-water fish as well. It just so happens to be goldfish he seeded in this neck of the woods. I can show you elsewhere that has fresh-water carp. None of those, however, are near any as convenient boiling pot; unless, of course, one has sprung up quite recently."

"Quite the possibility, from what you've said."

"You're remembering more and more about Saint-Georges. Good for you." His eyes sparked appreciative amusement. Obviously, he was having a good time.

Marie was having a good time, too. Charles was fun to be with, and each day she discovered she liked him (as well as loved him) more and more. If they had gotten off to a weird start, upon her arrival, well, then, they had surmounted initial obstacles and become stronger and closer because of them.

If only she knew what part Cécile played in her husband's life, things would have been nigh on perfect.

That particular day, though, she wasn't even tempted to ask her husband about Cécile, because she didn't want to spoil the moment. She just knew (her intuition again!) that any mention of Cécile would somehow throw a wrench in the present good mood of marital camaraderie.

"Ah, our lunch is already almost done," Charles observed, having pulled the fish out for a quick examination before returning it to the bubbling water. "Karena would be proud."

"I'll save my judgment until after the tasting, if you don't mind, thank you," Marie observed. She was, though, eager to taste it; the ride up the mountain had left her more than a little hungry.

Charles removed a knife from its sheath on his belt, and used it to help remove the fish from the cooking liquid. He let their beached meal momentarily drain of excess water before placing it on a rock, pool-side. With the knife's sharp blade, and his fingers, he skillfully removed the fins, cut off the head, and peeled off the skin. Then, cutting off the tail, he pinched the end portion of the reveled skeleton with the thumb and forefinger of his left hand and lifted the fish as he did so. He began working off the meat with the blade.

"They do this better in a restaurant, I know," he apologized with a sheepish grin. "So, be sure you watch for any small bones I've missed."

"We'd rather be at a loss for a doctor getting up here to rescue us from any fish bones caught in our throats, wouldn't we?" Marie smiled back, despite all of her efforts to sound serious. Certainly, she couldn't count upon Lucie and that old woman's two gladiators to come to the rescue a second time.

"Before our fine, dining, though...." Charles walked over to his saddlebag and produced salt and pepper shakers.

"You are full of surprises." Marie broke off a piece of unsalted fish in order to taste it before any seasoning. Actually, the flesh was already quite tasty, tender, and flaky. Or, possibly, she was just hungry enough to eat even a boiled shoe.

"I'm not quite through with surprises, yet, either," he said with evident glee. "So, don't go wolfing down this gourmet meal I've prepared until you see what additional goodies I'm capable of conjuring by way of our little rustic lunch, here, on our mountain."

Despite what he requested, Marie indulged with another piece of fish, concluding that it would likely have been just as tasty even if she weren't half starved. Its flesh was moist and had a pleasantly mild taste and texture. She tried to think of what other fish it reminded her of, and decided, finally, trout was the one that came closest.

"Just hold on, Miss Piggy," Charles said and got up. Instead of delving, again, into his saddlebag, he disappeared into a stretch of underbrush that completely overpowered the nearby small stream he'd recently, successfully, fished.

"You want me to put your fish in the warmer?" Marie called after.

"Funny!" he answered and appeared shortly with an ice bucket, complete with stream-cooled bottle of Dom Perignon in one hand and two tulip glasses in his other.

"You're kidding!" Marie laughed in evident pleasure. There was something about the very idea of volcano-boiled fish and mountain-stream cooled champagne, halfway up a jungle mountainside, which had all of the charm from which fictional love stories were made.

"After all, there is a limit to how much roughing it any civilized man can expect of his wife. Right? Right!" He handed Marie her glass, gently balancing his on the rock next to the fish. He popped the champagne cork and filled their glasses.

"You want to tell me how you managed this?" she asked, her champagne glass, rife with twirling small bubbles, in one hand, another piece of flavorful fish pinched within the thumb and fingers of her other.

"I had one of the natives bring it up a couple of days ago," he confessed, obviously pleased with his forethought.

"I shall confess, risking your head swelling up as big as a balloon, that it is, indeed, the perfect touch."

"Then, you must drink a toast with me to our love," he said, raising his glass. "You do know I love you, don't you?"

Marie couldn't help herself: she began to cry.

* * * * * * *

Afterwards, it was only too obvious they had been ridiculous to continue up the mountain, because the day would have been memorably perfect as it had stood. The lake in The Cauldron was bound to be anti-climactic, under the best of circumstances.

As it was, the euphoria Marie had felt building as she dined with her husband on fish and stream-cooled champagne, dissipated considerably as soon as the sun disappeared behind billowing curtains of damp fog. The mist wafted through the trees and settled like a shroud around horses and riders.

"It's cold," Marie said, never having expected it this chilly anywhere on Saint-Georges.

"I should have warned you that this sometimes happens," Charles apologized. "I've a couple of rain slickers in the saddlebag. They'll keep out the wet but not the chill."

"How much farther?" About the only thing she could see any longer was the path immediately in front of her horse. She had vision of her suddenly getting lost in the pea soup. How would a rescue party ever find her? She could have passed by Charles, no more than six feet between them, and never seen him.

"Not changing your mind, are you, honey?" His question sounded like a challenge, even if he hadn't intended it that way. "Getting cold feet, literally and figuratively?"

"I just pray you know where you're going, because I haven't a clue."

"Just be sure to say something every few minutes, so I'll know you're still with me." His little laugh indicated he was merely having a little fun at his wife's expense.

As much as she might genuinely have liked to be amused, Marie couldn't quite muster up much humor.

It was very easy for her to get the impression she and her horse weren't moving at all. The fog was all around them, cutting off not only her husband, for seemingly infinite minutes at a time, but, also, all the outside world.

"Shhhhhh!" Charles hissed just as Marie began to say something to let him know she was still there.

Marie's horse stopped automatically when her husband's horse did. At least, that was one advantage of being on the only trail that seemed readily available to them.

Marie wondered when Charles was going to quit hissing for silence, and, then, realized it was no longer her husband supplying the sound effects.

"What is it?" she asked. It sounded more and more like a gas leak.

"The possible reason why the haze is thicker today than usual," he said. "I figure a new cluster of steam vents has opened up somewhere dead ahead."

Marie blamed her shiver on the cold, but a closer analysis would have revealed she had been thinking of Father Westbrook at the exact moment her latest chill took root at the base of her spine and shivered on upward.

"Caused by the earthquake?" Marie spoke mainly to hear some other sound besides the breathless hissing.

"Donalds and Cromwell didn't report any new activity." Those were the two scientists who had returned to France after taking seismographic and other scientific readings. "They were up this way for several days running, if you remember."

"Maybe, we should head back down the mountain,"

Marie suggested tentatively.

"Let's take a closer look, first," he said. Then, possibly realizing his wife was getting unduly frightened, he reassured her. "There's nothing to worry about. As I've told you, before, these vents are always springing up, one day, only to disappear, the next."

He nudged his horse forward. Marie's horse automatically followed.

If possible, she thought the fog got denser. If possible, she found the air got warmer and wetter.

"Definitely, it sounds like steam vents!" Charles decided.

The muggy atmosphere played tricks with sound. Marie thought her husband was farther away than he was. For a moment, she had almost panicked; thankfully, before she did, she'd seen him through a sudden break in the mist.

The hissing got louder.

"Off through there, probably," Charles said; Marie sensed, rather than actually saw, in what direction he pointed. "We'd better not leave the trail, though."

Marie was pleased her husband's adventurous nature didn't tend toward the extreme. Also, she was pleased when the fog began to thin, and temperatures returned to pleasant.

Their arrival at the crater was, indeed, breathtaking, in that, just at that point, the fog blanket abruptly ended, the crater rim and the deep water below unveiled; the latter seemingly blue paint in a massive bowl edged with whipped cream. All of it was bathed in brilliant sunlight.

"It's about twenty miles around," Charles said. One look at Marie told him she was impressed, as he knew she would be, by the exceptional beauty of the panorama. "Before the big prehistoric boom, where we are is estimated to have been about two-thirds of the way up the mountain. The upper third blasted so far and wide into the upper atmosphere that a good inch of it settled in parts of Central and South America as topsoil."

"Decidedly beautiful!" she admitted.

"Glad you came?" He dismounted. "There's a way down to the water just over here."

The ground sloped to give a steep, but manageable, access to the lake edge. Across the way, however, cliffs rose to over two-thousand feet, making any approach to the water impossible from that direction.

Charles was already taking off his clothes for a swim when Marie and her horse joined him at the shoreline.

"Come on!" he invited. "Last one in...and all of that."

"You go ahead," Marie said. The visible crater rim reminded her of the gaping maw on all of those Fyrean carved amulets. As ridiculous as it seemed, even to her, she found the lake ominous in spite of its ethereal beauty. It was possibly made even more sinister *because* of its unworldly loveliness.

"Spoilsport!" Charles accused good-naturedly. His tanned skin exposed to the sun, he began his animated scamper along the rocks to climb atop one large slab of smooth black stone that extended, like a table, over the water's edge.

"Charles, do be careful," Marie warned, finding a spot and sitting down. "I'm counting on you to guide me back down the misty mountain, remember?"

As her husband exited the rock, in an impressively graceful swan dive, Marie saw the liquid into which he was about to enter suddenly begin to boil.

"Charles!" she screamed, too late, in warning.

* * * * * * *

She was hysterical. Not unusual, since she'd thought The Cauldron about to turn her husband into part of a giant stew.

How was she to know its bubbles were merely releases of benign subterranean gas?

"It's harmless, like the fizz in soda pop," Charles tried to explain, once he was safely out of the water and able to figure out what Marie had thought had happened. He hadn't known what to think when she'd let out her initial shriek which had caused him the painful belly-flop that had temporarily left him disoriented and winded.

"I thought for sure it was boiling! I thought it for sure!" she kept repeating. Knowing what he told her was undoubtedly the truth, considering he wasn't scalded, didn't erase how she'd felt when she'd seen him leave that rock and enter that water. She had felt so utterly helpless...helpless...helpless...helpless.

Truly, she had thought the man she loved was going to be boiled to death, like that fish they'd eaten earlier.

* * * * * * *

That night, after the trauma of The Cauldron, and after Charles' exhibited tenderness had convinced her he loved only her, she finally asked him about Cécile. She asked, because she was suddenly sure he would have the simple and harmless explanation that would put her needless fears and jealousies finally to rest; just as he had been able to explain away the bubbles in The Cauldron as nothing more than harmless gas.

She was wrong. She knew that the moment his body tensed beside hers on the bed.

"Who?" His voice was very guarded, calm only because he was so obviously making every conceivable effort to keep it that way. "What makes you think I know someone called Cécile?"

"You've mentioned her in your sleep," Marie said, but it was already obvious she'd be getting no answer. How could their love be expected to remain healthy when there were still secrets which couldn't be shared?

"I must have been dreaming about school," he said. "There used to be a girl called Cécile who sat next to me in chemistry class. She was the class brain. On the other hand, I was always afraid I was going to flunk out."

Marie didn't press him. She let his feeble explanation stand, even though she knew it for the lie it was.

She loved him, despite the lie, and she was positive, now, that he loved her. So what hold did this Cécile have on him that made that woman a secret he couldn't share with the wife he loved?

Even if Charles didn't seem to believe it, Marie believed their relationship was made of firm stuff. Knowing that, she was prepared to find out, once and for all, just who Cécile was, if just to put that particular bugbear to rest.

CHAPTER EIGHT
SECRETS REVEALED

If Saint-Georges resembled paradise, with its strands of white-sand beaches, green hills, verdant valleys, jutting mountain, and cascading fresh-water streams, then Isla Charlotte could only be described as hell, by comparison, in that it was little more than a mesa of black volcanic rock, thrust from the sea, and topped by an ugly colorless town constructed of stone blocks hewn from the very rocky upon which the town precariously squatted.

Carrying the analogy one step farther, Marie felt, during her boat trip to get there, like some poor soul making her journey across the River Styx, next stop Hades. If her resistance to seasickness had been low on the large steamer that had bought her to Saint-Georges, then it was virtually nonexistent on the small boat that took her to Isla Charlotte. The young, attractive youth, at the boat's helm, kept eyeing Marie as if she was a little out of her head...which she possibly was.

Marie suspected she had, just possibly, allowed her quest for an answer, regarding Cécile, to get the best of her. She hadn't been any too clever in her sleuthing, up until now, having come right out and asked Jannette what that girl knew. Jannette had tensed and clutched the talisman around her neck: a reaction Marie hadn't really unexpected, in that the girl, up until then, had seemed so level-headed and so unlikely to fall apart as easily as...say...Madeline had been expected to do.

Marie got little shivers when she thought of how Madeleine had reacted to the same query about Cécile. Marie's idea had been to scare the facts out of the nervous little parlor maid. Where Jannette had merely clammed up, like a mute, Madeleine had started running around the room like a chicken with her head cut off, waving her arms, and babbling an onrush of words Marie couldn't understand. The noise attracted every servant within hearing distance, all of whom must have thought someone was being murdered. As a result, there was no way news of the incident, and its cause, hadn't reach Charles who, when he heard, was quite livid.

"What kind of a woman sends a young servant girl into a fit of hysterics?" His face was beet red through his tan.

"How was I to know one question about Cécile would send her off like that?" Marie had countered.

"What is this phobia you have about Cécile, anyway?" He'd paced back and forth like a nervous jungle cat.

"Then, you're no longer denying there was a Cécile in your life!" Marie felt she might finally be getting somewhere. If so, then all of the fuss had been worth it.

"I don't recall ever denying it." His blue eyes had narrowed to mere slits.

"Back to the chemistry class story, are you?" So what that Marie had had the express opinion she was skating on thin ice?

"Cécile is dead if you must know!" he had snapped. "It would be best for all involved if you and everyone else let the poor girl rest in peace."

He had left Marie, and gone for the horseback ride which brought him back sweaty and un-talkative at supper time.

Back to being convinced her answers were never going to come from her husband (even though she had not lessened her resolve to have at them), Marie tried to be entirely charming and non-threatening throughout that evening meal. She'd figured Charles, as soon as he realized she'd dropped the subject, would return to his normal self. What convinced her otherwise was that he hadn't come to her suite that night—or any night since.

"I'm just restless, lately," he explained it away when she finally raised the subject of why they were back to separate bedrooms. "I don't like to disturb you."

Twice, Marie got up early to see Charles headed off across the back lawn with a bouquet of flowers. She identified those same bouquets, later, after he had ridden off to oversee the cacao planting, as having become part of the very same heap of decaying flowers Marie had spotted previously in the jungle, surrounded by small wooden amulets hanging from the branches of parenthesizing trees.

So, the way Marie saw it, her marriage was definitely on the skids, without her really knowing why. Since her sources seemed quickly to have dried up at the Château (not even Jannette coming through), Marie decided on looking for help from the only other person she knew in the vicinity...Pierre Yonne...if she didn't die from seasickness en route to see him.

As the tiny boat nosed toward the small harbor of Isla Charlotte, Marie found the island didn't improve any, by way of visual, when seen up close. If anything, nearness only made it all the more austere.

She thought she might persuade the young captain to wait, but he assured her there would be plenty of the locals willing to ferry her back for the same price she had paid him to get her there. So, she was no sooner on the small jetty than she was left stranded there.

Luckily, it didn't prove all that difficult to locate Pierre Yonne. There was only the one school on the island, and only the one teacher. Besides, it soon became apparent to Marie that everyone on Isla Charlotte pretty much knew everyone else who was present.

The harbor was a small natural shelter with moorings for the ten fishing boats that, aside from the occasional tourist, provided the majority of the island's economy. There were three storage warehouses around the water's edge, in one of which Marie found an overweight native, wearing what had to be a mile of bed sheet, who told her how to find Pierre.

To reach the top of the island required boarding a tram that creaked its way at a snail's pace, all of the while threatening to break free. It ran via a maze of belts, wheels, and pulleys. When the power generator went off, which was more often than not, mules were attached to the cable mechanism and did the job just as well, if not better.

From the top of the rock, Marie had a good view back toward Saint-Georges and Mont d'Esnembuc.

Pierre's students were at recess, their teacher at his desk and relaxing in one of his rare moments of peace and quiet during the school day. He'd just finished a chapter in the novel, *Incident at Brimzinsky*, he was reading (one of countless paperbacks he always brought back with him from his holidays in the States). As the sun shone directly in through the open door, casting Marie in complete silhouette, it was impossible for him to identify her, even after she spoke.

"I suppose you don't remember me," Marie had said. She had realized the triteness of that introduction, but she couldn't think of anything else more adequately to fit the bill. She was, however, a little disappointed when he genuinely seemed not to remember her. "From the ship. I'm Marie Camaux."

He got quickly to his feet, approaching her from an angle that finally allowed him to bring her out of concealing shadow.

"Of course, I remember, Madam Camaux!" he assured. "The light incoming with you through the door was what kept me from it. Whatever brings you here? I'm afraid our accommodations are a little more rustic than you're probably used to on the big island."

He commandeered a chair for her during his running commentary. When she was comfortably seated, he disappeared outside the building for a few moments.

"I sent the beasties home for the day," he said, returning shortly. He seemed younger than Marie remembered. Also, she remembered his hair more brown than its present attractive shade of blond. Possibly, the sun (the island seemed to have precious few trees) had been busy bleaching his strands to their present lighter shade. "It's so very seldom I get a visitor, I figure the occasion, now come, sees me deserving the rest of the day off."

"You won't get into trouble, will you?" she ventured. "About sending the children home early, I mean."

"We run a loose ship over here. Besides, everyone knows if I ever get in any kind of snit, they would have a hard time finding any quick replacement. This doesn't exactly look like a teacher's Shangri-la, does it? I figure, I'll stick it out another year, until my contract runs out. After that, I've an offer from a school in Villeneuve."

"Maybe, then, you'll be able to drop by for that promised visit."

"Actually, I thought of coming over on several different occasions," Pierre admitted, smiling guiltily. "Then, I figured it might be well to let the newlyweds settle in a bit before I forced them into entertaining a mere acquaintance. Then, the earthquake came, and I had more good intentions of making sure you'd weathered the storm, but word crossed over that all was well.

After which...." He left it at that.

Marie smiled.

"The road to hell is always paved with good intentions, yes?" Pierre additionally excused. Actually, he'd simply decided Mr. and Mrs. Camaux were in a totally different social league from his, and he'd immediately talked himself out of calling, each and every time the idea had seriously come to mind.

"So, if Muhammad isn't coming to the mountain, the mountain must come to Muhammad," Marie said. She flashed Pierre another of her best smiles. If she wanted this man's help, it was important he like her, although it seemed fairly obvious he already did. Then, again, maybe his obvious delight in seeing her was no more than the typical reaction he would have had to anyone showing up on this God-forsaken bit of land in the Caribbean.

"How about a little stroll?" he suggested. "I'll show you the island's high points. That should take us all of five minutes." He laughed. "Then, I know a spot, right beneath one of the few trees that have managed to somehow take root on this rock pile, where we can get a cool glass of liquid refreshment."

"My husband is frankly surprised everyone here hasn't already packed up and moved over to the bigger island," Marie said, finding the heat was kept from being totally oppressive, once, again, outside, only by a cool breeze that came up from the sea and across the mesa-like summit.

"Most of the young people do move off when they

get old enough," Pierre admitted. He held to Marie's left arm to steady her, since there were no sidewalks or paving. "The older ones swear they've been saved once already and refuse to tempt Fyrea's wrath again." He lowered his voice to an amused whisper, even though there was no one but her to hear. "Everyone, you know, is quite convinced that mountain of yours is about to let go with one big bang. Every earthquake that has happened during the last hundred years has only strengthened those beliefs. When a family has been burned once, it gets a little leery about trying its luck again in one and the same place. I suppose you've heard of the big-island village that got run over by the lone lava flow in 1901. Well, the inhabitants of that village decided it was safer to set up housekeeping here, or you probably wouldn't find me here teaching their children and grandchildren."

"I heard the village was empty at the time," Marie said. She saw a tree up ahead and hoped it was "the" tree at which they were planning to stop. As far as she was concerned, she had already seen as much of Isla Charlotte as she, or anyone else, could ever possibly care to see.

"Oh, the village was empty, all right," Pierre said, delighted to have fresh ears to hear a very well-worn story. "That was because a psychic local girl showed up to warn the inhabitants away. Luckily, they believed her, or it would have ended up final curtains for the lot of them."

"You believe that story, do you?" Marie asked, hardly

thinking it possible that he did. "I mean about the girl having foretold the eruption. We had a couple of scientists at the house recently who said it's hard even for them, with all of their modern scientific equipment, to predict just when, or if, any given mountain plans to blow its top."

Pierre shrugged.

Marie was heartened by the sight of a kiosk and several empty tables set up in the shade ahead.

"The animals know such things," Pierre said. "I heard the birds took flight before the latest earthquake began."

Marie remembered the sight she'd had of them as they rose out of the trees into the darkness of the night. Would she, in fact, ever forget?

"I've heard it said some scientists believe we all had just such second sight as those birds, at one time, civilization having dulled our natural capacity to call upon it," Pierre continued.

They reached the tree. Pierre pulled out one of the chairs in the shade and waited until Marie was seated before he sat across the small table from her. He ordered lemonade for both of them.

"She's still wandering around over there, you know," he said, taking their drinks from the young native boy who had just managed to deliver them in the process of spilling a good bit on the ground. Pierre passed Marie's glass off to her.

"Who is?" Marie asked. She'd momentarily lost the gist of their conversation, more caught up in trying to decide if the hygiene of this particular establishment warranted her chancing any actually drinking of the drink.

"The psychic who warned off the villagers. As a matter of fact, I'm sure you must have run into her; an old woman by now. Her people used to be owned by your husband's people, back in the days when slave labor made all of the wheels turn around here."

Marie, thirsty, took a sip of her lemonade. Her thoughts were no longer on how clean or dirty the glass was.

"Lucie Bruay," Pierre surprised.

"Lucie Bruay, a psychic?" Marie asked; her glass down on the table. Her eyes were intent upon Pierre across from her.

"She's direct-line from some of the original island stock. From back when it wasn't Saint-Georges but some unpronounceable pagan name. Actually, I guess Lucie is now the only one left of the indigenous tribe. Most were killed off in the first days of French settlement. Worked to death, quite frankly. When they were used up, the French brought in the Negroes. By the way, feel free to interchange psychic with priestess, or witch doctor, or diviner, or conjurer, or any number of other as likely apt terms. Not that old Lucie goes around casting spells on anybody, mind you, as you've likely very well noted. From what I hear, she's never done anybody any harm but has done an awfully lot of good. As for her daughter, you and I know that's a completely different...."

He stopped mid-sentence, realizing he had possibly approached the bounds of conversational good taste, forgetting himself because it was so seldom possible for him to engage in enjoyable conversation with anyone. If he was interested in getting some first-hand facts from Marie (Pierre, after all, had been in the States when the scandal had happened), he resisted the temptation. She was an influential woman to have as a friend. For that matter, her husband was even more influential. There was little point in alienating either wife or husband by letting Marie know Pierre was well aware of certain rumors regarding skeletons in the Camaux closets.

"Her daughter?" Marie asked. "Lucie Bruay has a daughter?"

Pierre wondered if it was really possible that Marie didn't have a clue, as she pretended.

"*Had* is the key tense. The girl died a few months back." He decided to leave it at that.

However, Marie was curious to know more.

"Died how?"

Pierre delivered a noncommittal shrug and decided it was time he shifted the conversation elsewhere. He should never have guided it in that particular direction.

"You didn't come all of this way to hear me spout a bunch of superstitious nonsense," he said. "You must have come for some very specific reason. For, you'll note, I've not flattered myself into believing it was just me that brought you over that seasickness-producing channel of water."

"You remember my rather green-around-the-gills complexion the last time you saw me, do you?" Marie bantered, although she had all intentions of pumping him for more information on Lucie Bruay and Lucie's dead daughter.

She took another sip of lemonade.

"Actually, I need your help," she said.

"Sure. Anything I can do." He wondered what kind of help Marie Camaux could possibly want from him.

"Your next trip over to Saint-Georges, I'd like you to ask around about a certain woman. I've done a little research on my own, but I've been unable to come up with all that much."

"I would think your best bet would be to hire a private detective." Pierre was suddenly very leery. There was no way he wanted to choose sides if Charles and Marie Camaux were already pairing off over another woman.

"Oh, it's nothing like I probably have you thinking," Marie said, giving a *don't-be-silly* laugh. "I have no suspicions at all that my husband is cheating on me. Actually, the woman in question is, I believe, like Lucie's daughter, dead."

"Dead?"

"I'm embarrassed to admit that's about all I've been able to find out about her. That, and, of course, that her name is...was...Cécile."

Marie was a little uncertain just what could be read in the expression that suddenly crossed Pierre's face.

"That's all you know?" Pierre managed finally. "Her name is Cécile, and she's likely dead. Nothing more?"

"I'm afraid that's it," Marie admitted with an apologetic smile. "Not really very much for anyone to go on, I know, but I thought, maybe, you, since you've done so much research into the area's history, might be more successful than I've been."

"Can I ask just why you're so interested in this woman?"

"I've heard several servants mention her, in passing, but every time they see me, they clam up," Marie out-and-out lied.

Pierre could very well imagine why servants might go mute, especially if Charles Camaux kept his wife in the dark about Cécile.

"I suspect she might have been one of my husband's old flames," Marie said.

Pierre took another swallow of his drink. The liquid was going warm in the glass.

"Her full name was Cécile Bruay," he said finally. "Other than that, I'm afraid I can't help you."

In the end, though, he told her most of what he knew, which—he kept impressing upon her—was purely hearsay, since he hadn't been a confident of any of the parties involved; he hadn't even been on the island at the time.

Maybe, he told her as much as he did, because he was simply a sucker for any woman who cried, and Marie had quickly broken into tears.

Maybe he told her, because he truly believed she was out to save her marriage that she sincerely believed to be on the rocks because of secrets kept from her about a woman now dead.

Maybe he told her simply because he liked her, and he found it frankly ridiculous that she should be brought to so much unhappiness by a bunch of superstitious folderol that any sensible man, like Charles Camaux, should have been able to identify as the claptrap it really was.

That is, if Charles was capable, anymore, of comprehensive reasoning. The rumor was, after all, that Cécile Bruay had drugged him, using certain recipes learned at her mother's knee. She had, then, seduced him, and had somehow connived to have some Catholic priest perform a marriage ceremony. Then, suddenly, she was dead, her body spirited away by natives to some jungle burial plot before there could be an official autopsy.

The local goddess-of-the-volcano, Fyrea, supposedly had been very unhappy that the daughter of Her chief priestess, Lucie, had given more intense worship to a man than to Her. So, Fyrea had supposedly cursed Cécile to an early grave, as well as cursed Charles to perish in the same flames as those with which Fyrea intended, very soon, to kill most everyone on Saint-Georges.

The French community, of course, believed Lucie Bruay, adamantly against the marriage of her daughter to Charles Camaux, might have actually gone so far as to do away with her own daughter.

* * * * * * *

Marie sat in the bow of the boat, looking back toward

Pierre at the outboard motor. She wasn't really seeing him. She wasn't focusing, either, on Isla Charlotte which was fading from foreground to background as the craft neared the Saint-Georges coastline.

Her thoughts were turned inward, trying to decide how she was going to take what she now knew and use it to save her marriage.

The trouble was, as Pierre had successfully pointed out to her, all of what he had told her was purely scuttle-butt. As the most prominent landholder on the island, Charles Camaux was always talked about. There was bound to be whispers of intrigue and scandal. Just because a thing was said, didn't mean it was Gospel. In fact, it might be an out and out lie, or even a half-truth.

What, though, if Cécile *had,* against the will of her mother and Fyrea, conspired to marry Charles? What if she *had* resorted to some form of native herb, drug, or witchcraft, feeding it to Charles in his food or drink? Wasn't there, then, the possibility that certain aftereffects from that could still linger in his system, causing him to confuse Marie at times with the dead and buried Cécile? His erratic behavior could, in that context, be rationalized. Likewise, it could be very clear as to why Charles would be disturbed by Marie's continual attempts to bring up Cécile. His thoughts of her would likely be confusing and seemingly best forgotten. The chances were very good he was even unaware of what he had said and had done during his relapses. Not remembering, wasn't it logical for him to be unable to grasp why Marie had suddenly developed such a need to know all there was to know about the manipulative Cécile?

Did Charles even know he'd been drugged?

Did Charles even remember his marriage to Cécile was performed by Father Westbrook?

On the other hand, there were several aspects of the rumors which Marie found harder to believe.

Take the notion that Charles was entangled within some kind of ju-ju native curse, based on a pagan religion that had Lucie Bruay as its chief priestess, Charles scheduled for death in some kind of volcanic upheaval scheduled for Saint-Georges by a vengeful goddess. While it could be argued that he had been drawn back to the island, after having first tried to flee to England (where he had met and married Marie), it could, also, be rationalized that he had returned for simpler reasons. Saint-Georges was his home. He had been born and raised there. His parents, grandparents, and a whole gamut of his kin were buried there. His roots went deep into its volcanic soil. Why shouldn't he prefer his island home to island England, or to anywhere else in the world for that matter?

Curses and all of that were for primitive societies still clinging to old superstitions and beliefs. This was the twenty-first century, and Charles was a twenty-first-century man with the best education money could buy. Once made effective by ignorance and fear, curses were now destined to dissolve quickly within modern-day enlightenment.

Yet, there were still isolated incidences of intelligent men succumbing to curses placed on them by voodoo priests in places like Haiti. If Charles had been confused by drugs, his mind might have been overly susceptible to suggestion, no matter how absurd that suggestion might have been.

Marie firmly refused to believe Lucie Bruay would kill her own daughter, no matter what the malicious tongues were wagging to the contrary; no matter how much Marie continued to dislike the old hag.

She had seen Lucie working with the sick and the injured, in the aftermath of the earthquake, and, now, knew that Lucy had warned a whole village out of the way of an exploding volcano. It seemed inconceivable that such an altruistic woman, so intent on saving lives and relieving misery, could have stooped to taking another person's life—let alone the life of her own daughter.

More likely, Cécile hadn't limited her drug experiments to the food and drink she gave Charles and was, herself, dead of a chemical overdose. If Lucie had been part of the plot which had stolen Cécile's body for jungle burial, then who could condemn a mother for wanting her daughter's body left undefiled by a coroner's scalpel?

All in all, Marie felt far better equipped to cope, now that she had a workable outline—no matter how much of that outline would eventually turn out to be based on sheer rumor. She no longer could blame Charles for not telling her things which—more than likely—he couldn't even sort out in his own mind.

Cécile was dead. Cécile was buried.

Marie felt confident she could eventually win any battle with a dead woman for the possession of Charles Camaux.

When the effects of whatever it was Cécile had fed Charles' bloodstream began to fade all the more (Marie refused to contemplate the possibility that there would always be some kind of permanent residue), then, Charles and Marie would only find their love strengthened because of what they had been through together.

Marie hadn't had to drug Charles to get him. She didn't need to drug him to keep him. Her love had gotten him. Her love would keep him.

Suddenly, she felt better and less troubled than she had in a very long time.

"I'm not even seasick," she told Pierre who, up until then, had been concerned by Marie's intense introspection.

"The water is calmer than I've ever seen it through here," Pierre said. "Without a motor, we'd stall for sure."

Marie was crossing a stretch of ocean that could have passed for the glass-like lake in The Cauldron.

* * * * * * *

Pierre didn't dock the boat in Villeneuve.

"If you don't mind the walk, I was told of a shortcut that can save you your winding car ride," he'd said when he'd emerged from the squat building on Isla Charlotte where he'd gone to borrow the boat to take

Marie back to Saint-Georges.

He steered the craft into a small deserted cove, complete with its own stretch of white sand, where he successfully beached it and helped Marie out without even getting her feet wet.

"Now, if I haven't been led down the garden path, by the old salt who told me, there should be a trail some-where over...there!" He pointed. "So far, so good. Now, we're supposed to be able to see the Château from the top of the initial upgrade. The trail should come out right on the leading edge of your front lawn. Your husband's grandfather, I was told, once had some kind of a boat docked here. I'll walk you home, though, just to make sure you get there safely."

"Really, you've been more than kind enough already," Marie said. "I've had a horse as far as the top of the bluff and know the way from here."

"You're sure? It doesn't seem all that gentlemanly simply to drop a beautiful woman off in some strange stretch of wilderness."

"In this case, I assure you, it's quite the most gentle-manly thing to do," Marie said. "I'd prefer a little private time to myself, to think things through, anyway. You understand?"

"You wouldn't lie about knowing your way home from here?"

"I assure you, I have no more desire to see me wandering around lost than you do."

"Well, then...." Pierre could think of nothing better to add; so, he shrugged and slapped his hands against his thighs.

"Thank you, Pierre...for everything."

"I almost didn't tell you the gossip; you know that, don't you?"

"I appreciate your reluctance to spread idle rumor about my husband. This time, however, you were wise to make the exception, I promise you."

"So, come back to Isla Charlotte later and let me know how things work out, will you?"

"You must try making it to the Château," Maria said, taking his hand and squeezing it. "I'm sure you and my husband will hit it off. Certainly, you're the first real friend I've found in my new home."

He gave a delightful blush and headed back to the boat. Marie waited until he had pushed off and was afloat, and, then, she turned and headed up the slope.

The trail was steep and hard going at first. On horseback, earlier in the week, Marie had decided it was too steep to head down. Going up on foot, though, she managed, although she was panting hard when she reached the leveling off point.

She looked, first, toward the Château, seeing its familiar chimneys off through the trees in the distance. Then, she looked back over the water to where Pierre was circling the boat to await her signal—just in case the house hadn't turned out to be where they both thought it was, or steam vents had reared their nasty heads by way of a blockade.

Marie waved assurances that she was sufficiently oriented to carry on from there. Pierre waved back before steering his boat for open water.

Marie sat down for a moment to catch her breath and to watch Pierre's progression out through the mouth of the cove. The ocean was still smooth as glass, as if calmed by oily slick. There was hardly any evidence of the small boat's movement, as if all signs were erased on the slate as quickly as they were drawn there.

When the boat was a mere dot, Marie stood and stretched, enjoying the release of tension along her vertebrae-popping spine. She turned toward the Château, hearing and seeing the birds at one and the same time.

Majestically, they rose in one giant mass, circling and veering out to sea.

With a strange and eerie sense of déjà-vu, Marie watched them go, feeling the coldness brought to her veins by the sight. The impression was no less awesome for having, this time, occurred during daylight. Where before, it had appeared merely a black and shadowy mass, it was now an obvious undulating wave of varied-colored birds by way of a very knowing population deserting Saint-Georges—for safety?

Out at sea, Pierre saw the massive flock pass over him. As Marie watched from the bluff, she saw his boat make the wide turn back toward Saint-Georges. Pierre knew what was happening, as much as she did, and he was coming back for her. There might, after all, still be time for her to rush down the hill, climb into the boat, and sail out to sea, before....

Before the earthquake? Or would it be something

worse, this time?

"Don't be a fool!" she screamed to Pierre in the distance who obviously couldn't hear her. She couldn't wait for him to get within shouting distance, either. She didn't have the time, not knowing how much time she did have. Her place was with her husband. She wouldn't leave Charles, even had she known for certain there was safety for her in that returning boat with her friend.

She started running through the forest and its underbrush toward the distant Château.

CHAPTER NINE
WHEN SHALL WE THREE MEET AGAIN?

The first tremor was a faint vibration felt only against the soles of Marie's running feet. It passed, and, then, returned even less intense. It disappeared completely, and then returned, only to disappear again.

Marie felt like a mouse who knew she was being played with by a clever cat that tried to lull her into a false sense of complacency. Something big was building, though, and Marie could feel "it" in the air, couched within the trees, buried within the earth. She sensed it within in the wide expanses of sea and sky, both so blue that they were almost too painful for her eyes to see.

Whatever it was, it chose to build in complete silence, sneaking up on her. It was mainly Marie's own loud breathing that she heard, not any outward noises or sounds that relayed any sense of impending disaster. She was panting for air, her lungs heaving as she worked them to capacity. Her chest cavity hurt. Her throat hurt. Her legs hurt. Yet, she ran and continued to do so until she could run no farther—only to continue running even then.

Until, it was the ground suddenly come up to meet Marie's falling foot, instead of vice versa. Amid a loud cacophony that was painful to the ears, Marie lost her balance. Her right side no sooner hit the ground (knocking out what precious little wind she had left), than the ground dropped from beneath her.

Like a rag doll tossed upon a blanket, Marie was thrown upward into nothing but air all around her. This made the ground even harder the next time it found her.

* * * * * * *

It was quiet, though not a relaxed quiet. It was a fake calm pregnant with tensions not yet released. It was a mere pause, obviously not a finish.

Marie groaned.

Was there one part of her body that didn't ache?

She'd lost all sense of time. Hours could have passed, or mere seconds. Her watch, broken and stopped at 3:15 (A.M.? P.M?), insinuated a possible passage of only a few minutes.

She came to her hands and knees, starting with fright when a nearby tree, jarred loose in the shake, commenced its belated fall with a crashing thud that would have sounded loud even had there been no one there to hear it.

Marie's knees were scratched and bleeding. Her right arm was numb; she vaguely remembered hitting her crazy bone. Her dress was torn. She tasted blood and realized she'd bitten her lip.

Slowly, she managed to get to her feet, mentally checking for broken bones.

She started off, again, each step revealing new aches and pains. That said...she wasn't dead. She was still moving and still able to glimpse distant Château chimneys through the trees (thank God, the building was still standing!). She would be home...eventually.

What if no one was there? They could have all fled during the time it took Marie to reach them though the interfering jungle. Even Charles might be gone. There would have been no reason for him to wait for her, thinking her still on Isla Charlotte visiting with her schoolteacher friend.

She was close to panic when she finally did burst free of underbrush and onto Château lawn. As in the previous earthquake, a canyon-like trench had opened in the grass, only this time it had remained open, revealing insides of iron-red earth, root-strewn and speckled with rocks and boulders, the latter often the size of small houses. Eerily, she half expected the once-swallowed butler, Marc, to climb on out.

She ran parallel to the trench, keeping well away from it. She still remembered, only too well, the way the sides had previously collapsed like quicksand.

Where the abyss finally came together, a visible crack still continued its run almost to the Château steps.

There was a hazy cast to the air which Marie recognized as not entirely from dust. Somewhere, close by, steam vents had sprouted to life and were venting their foul-smelling sulfuric super-heated fumes...with accompanying hisses.

There was no indication of life.

The Château doors were open, but the foyer immediately beyond was vacant.

"Charles!"

Marie told herself not to panic. Even if Charles wasn't there, even if Pierre had decided Marie wasn't returning to the boat so had headed back to Isla Charlotte, there were other alternatives available to her. There were several cars kept in the garage. Surely, one or two of them had been left. If not, there were the horses. If the horses had been turned out to better fend for themselves, Marie still had her legs.

"Charles!"

This upheaval had been worse than the last one, evidenced by the large crack now visible in the side of the walk-in fireplace; a large hunk of mantle stone had dropped into the middle of the hearth.

"Charles!"

She walked to the den and slid open the door, giving a small gasp of surprise to find Lucie Bruay seated, like some kind of regal mummy, in one of the large wing-back chairs facing the doorway.

"It's happening!" the old woman said, frightening Marie who had thought the old woman possibly dead.

"Have you seen my husband?" Marie asked. Even though the old woman might sense Marie's presence, her eyes focused on something far more distant. Her pupils, entirely independent of one another, began, disconcertingly, to wander in spasmodic jerks.

"Are you prepared to die?" Lucie asked in a macabre whisper.

As if on cue, the ground moved.

Marie backed into the rectangle formed by the nearest doorjamb, preparing to flee if the quake got more forceful. Although the Château had survived at least two big quakes, since Marie's arrival on the island, its tons of rock could still fall at any minute. If and when they did, Marie had no intention of being buried beneath them.

The ground movement suddenly ceased as quickly as it had begun.

"My husband?" Marie tried again. "Have you seen Charles?"

With a sudden jolt, like two grapes on a slot machine clicking into adjoining spots, Lucie's eyes focused. Her small, pinpoint pupils came alive with genuine recognition of Marie in the room.

"Your husband, my daughter's husband," she said. "Do you know where my daughter is this night?"

"Where is my husband?" Marie cared absolutely nothing about where Lucie's daughter might be, only wondering why there was any need to bother with this uncooperative old crone when Charles might still possibly be somewhere in the house.

"What do you care where he is or isn't?" Lucie asked, sitting straighter, clamping her fingers into the arms of the chair, like a bird's talons skewered its prey. "Fyrea will have him. He took what wasn't his for the taking—my daughter. Did he tell you that, Madame Camaux, Marie Camaux, the second Mrs. Charles Camaux? For that, he must suffer the consequences, just as my daughter did."

"Your daughter tricked him!" Marie accused. "She used drugs that *you* taught her how to use, making you as guilty as she was."

"Heard that, did you?" Lucie asked. She gave a frown that wrinkled her already wrinkled face into even more wrinkles.

"Deny it!" Marie challenged

"Mmmmmm," Lucie mumbled noncommittally. Her eyes unfocused, yet again, and commenced a simultaneous slow roll into the back of her head. Spittle foamed at the right corner of her mouth.

Marie knew she could get nowhere with a woman who, difficult in normal circumstances, had obviously lost her senses. She turned to begin a search of the house.

Charles stood not two feet behind her.

"Charles, thank heavens!"

She ran into his open arms, holding him, sobbing against his chest. Except for a scratch along his right cheek, and several rips in his shirt, he looked unhurt.

He held her close, bringing his right hand to the back of her head to comb his fingers through her hair.

"We did this, you know?" he whispered, his voice a low, soothing caress. "We did this, and now we're reaping the just rewards for our folly."

Marie pulled back sharply, knowing her husband

wasn't talking to her, but, once again, conversing with the dead Cécile Bruay.

"*Digliji,*" Lucie Bruay said; Marie momentarily thought the old woman back to mumbling gibberish.

At that moment, though, Lucie was quite lucid. Her eyes were directly on Marie.

"That was the plant my daughter used to drug your husband," Lucie elucidated.

At the window, Charles stood, gazing out on a scene that looked plagiarized from Dante's *Inferno*. The air was thick with smoke and steam, and it smelled of fire and brimstone.

"The plant in question grows high on the mountain," Lucie continued, "in an area usually shrouded in mist. It's for use only in highly religious ceremonies. My daughter committed sacrilege by using it otherwise. Then, she was never one to hold to the old ways. She wanted new and material things of the kind only someone as rich and influential as Charles Camaux could give her. It made little difference that he didn't love her. What a price, though, she had to pay for such folly, make him pay, make you pay, make us all pay."

"Charles, you, and I have to get out of here," Marie insisted. "If we don't leave soon, we'll be dead—if just from asphyxiation."

"I'm old," Lucie answered. "I am, in fact, *very* old. What do I care, any more, of living?"

"Well, I'm not old," Marie insisted. "Neither is Charles!

"Run, then, if you think there's a way for you out of

here," Lucie said. "As for your husband, well, as you can see, he waits to pay his dues."

"Pay his dues for what?" Marie wanted to know. She told herself not to panic. There had to be a way out of this, somehow, even though a meandering river of magma already could be seen oozing down one of the valleys to cut off the road to Villeneuve. "By your own admission, it was your daughter who did the deed."

"There is nothing I can do for your husband," Lucie said with a shrug. "As you have seen, reality has once more escaped him."

"I won't let him die! Do you hear me?"

"If Fyrea wants him dead, She'll have him," Lucie stated with unarguable finality, "just as She's had my daughter."

Marie went to Charles by the window. She took his arm and gave it a forceful tug to pull him around to face her.

"Charles, listen to me!" she shouted. "If we don't get out of here, and soon, we are all going to be toast. Are you going to stand there and let that happen?"

"Cécile...."

"I am *not* Cécile! Nor have I ever been. Cécile is dead! Cécile is buried!"

"Cécile...."

"IS DEAD! IS DEAD! IS BURIED!"

He looked confused. Marie could only hope she was, somehow, getting through to him.

"I'm Marie, your wife, Charles. Do you want me to die, because I'm not going to move one step out of this house without you? If we don't leave together, we're going to end up as dead, together, as this crazy old lady, over there, is going to end up dead with her daughter." She'd pointed to Lucie.

"Marie?" Charles asked as if buried deep in the ground, calling up though the smallest of air holes in his casket.

"We...have...got...to...get...out of here, Charles," Marie insisted. She gripped both of his biceps and gave a hearty shake that jarred her teeth while hardly budging her husband's muscled body.

"We can't get out," he told her. "The lava already blocks the road."

"We'll take the horses," Marie said, "and go around the lava."

"I've turned the horses loose," he said. This was something Marie had surmised earlier. Still, if nothing else, she took heart in the fact that his mind was apparently once again functioning in the present.

"Then, we'll just have to walk out of here," she said, hoping he could get himself enough together to make a more viable suggestion than that. "Well walk to the cove where Pierre Yonne has a boat waiting."

No way did she believe Pierre would still be waiting, even if he had returned all of the way to shore. On the other hand, she felt if she could just get Charles started into doing something—anything—his natural instincts for survival were bound to kick in.

"Pierre Yonne?" he asked; his expression gave the impression he was genuinely searching his memory for a way to put a face to the name.

"You don't know him, but I do, Charles," Marie said. "He's from Isla Charlotte and has his boat in a cove not too far away that can get us to safety."

"Likely story!" Lucie Bruay huffed, screwing up her nose in disdain.

"Shut up!" Marie commanded and turned back to Charles.

His eyes seemed brighter. He rubbed the side of his jaw like a man just hit and trying to come out of the resulting stun.

"Pierre is waiting with his boat, Charles. Really he is. I can't get there by myself, though, because I'm too weak and too frightened. You have to come with me."

"I can't," he said. "I have to stay here and wait."

"Wait for what?" Marie asked in furious frustration. "The only thing you're going to find here is death, and you don't really want to die. You don't really want me to die with you, do you?"

"I must," he said, shaking his head to clear it of haze which wasn't just inside it but floating the air in result of the conflagration in progress outside.

"Why must you die, Charles? Why?"

"She said so," Charles said, glancing toward Lucie who eyed both of them from the chair.

"What does *she* know?" Marie asked, feeling she was definitely making headway.

She was encouraged that his past spells always ended, eventually, followed each time by longer stretches of rationality. If she could shake him free of this one, she was sure things would turn out all right.

"Fyrea would have me," Charles said. He nodded in Lucie's direction. "She said it was so."

"If Fyrea *really* wants you, Charles, do you really think She won't get you, whether you stay here or try to get me to safety? Isn't doing something better than just waiting like a sacrificial lamb destined for slaughter? Well, isn't it?"

"Who's Pierre?" Charles asked. "Some man you've been seeing on the sly?"

His eyes sparkled, and there was just a definitive trace of embarrassment within the slight grin on his lips.

"Charles, is it really you? Is it?"

"By the looks of things, we are in a pretty mess, here," he said. "We're going to have to move very fast if we plan to get out."

"Oh, Charles!" Marie exclaimed, sobbing her relief. She fell into his arms, gathering comfort beyond belief from his very nearness.

This was her Charles! This was her man! She had, with persistence, triumphed over Cécile, and Lucie, and brought back to reality the man she loved.

"One thing I don't need right now, it's an hysterical wife," he said, his mouth spreading into a wide smile, while his eyes flashed genuine concern for their situation. "Promise me you're not going to fall to pieces on me at this stage of the game."

"I promise," she said, quickly wiping away her tears of joy. "I do, I do, I do...truly promise."

* * * * * * *

They stopped from pure exhaustion. Smoke burned their eyes and throats. Branches had striated their arms and faces with whip and burn marks during their mad dash thorough a jungle often in flames.

"You're both fools!" Lucie Bruay spat as Charles squatted to put her unceremoniously on the ground. Against Lucie's great protest, and Marie's uncertainty, Charles had carried the old woman from the Château with them. "We can, none of us, escape the wrath of Fyrea. The least we might have done was waited gracefully for our end in the relative comfort of the Château."

"I can't believe a feisty old woman like you can really want to go out without a fight," Charles said, his sentence punctuated by the resounding boom of thunder.

Ominous clouds were piled in an increasingly impressive crown atop Mont d'Esnembuc. Lightning flashed with more and more regularity, turning the growing twilight to full day.

"Fools! Foolish fools!" Lucie muttered.

Charles turned his attention to his wife.

"You do know the chances are slim that your friend is still going to be there, in the cove, with his boat," he said, shaking his head.

"I know," Marie admitted.

"Even so, they're the best odds we seem to have at the moment. Heading any other way would have us fenced in by lava flows."

"Best to go out with a fight, isn't that what you said?"

He gave her a kiss at the exact moment a gust of wind blew a sheet of hot smoke to engulf them. They came apart, coughing.

"Time to move on, Lucie," Charles said, taking hold of the old woman's feather-weight body and lifting.

Lucie started coughing; managing to stop only after Charles was, once again, running with her through the smoke-filled jungle.

"Fools!" Lucie muttered indignantly, suspecting that if Fyrea didn't soon kill her, the mad rush through the flaming forest was liable to do just as good a job.

* * * * * * *

Marie didn't remember the cove as being quite so far. Maybe, that was because her return to it was filled with so many detours necessitated by the myriad ravages The Cauldron's eruption made upon the landscape. Everywhere, there were great geysers of steam spewing out of the ground, or pools of liquid bubbling viscous goo. The human trio was continually faced with gaping chasms, too great to jump. There was the fire, the heat, the blinding and suffocating smoke. Meanwhile, the grumbling mountain continually insinuated it hadn't yet finished all it planned to do.

The earth began a new series of shimmies and shakes. As long as the rolling of the ground remained minor, Marie could continue, having become somehow as accustomed to the movement as a sailor became eventually adjusted to the flux of the sea beneath his ship.

When the ground groaned, buckled, and gave massive heaves that were impossible to ride out, though, there was very little the trio could do except go down and pray the bucking would soon stop, and hope, against hope, that one of the increasing number of toppling trees wouldn't decide to fall on top of them.

When the gauntlet was finally run successfully, the three panting their ragged gasps for breath to bring little else into their lungs but hot, smoke-saturated air, they found what had been a possibility all along was, in fact, reality: Pierre Yonne and his boat weren't there.

Marie felt sick to her stomach, knowing she had secretly held out hope for Pierre and rescue by him, no matter what the odds against it. That hope had kept her going when she had thought she'd no strength left. Now what? They might as well have been back at the Château. While Isla Charlotte was out there, obscured by the haze, it might as well have been halfway around the world without any feasible way to reach it.

"Fools, fools, pathetic fools!" Lucie muttered, trying to settle as best she could against the rock where Charles propped her upon letting her down. Her bones had been so jolted, in Charles' arms, that they now provided one huge ache that failed to escape any part of her body.

"Shut up! Shut up! Shut up!" Marie insisted.

For a very long minute, Charles simply held Marie close and waited for her nerves to calm, which they eventually did.

"Feel better?" he asked, giving her a grin.

Despite their nearness to the ocean, there was no relief from the increasing heat. The air became very much like that of a blast furnace, turning their faces red and sweaty.

Charles ripped off the tail of his shirt and went to the water's edge, dipping the material into the salty liquid. The ocean was warm, heated from the tons of lava The Cauldron poured into it at several points along the island's shoreline.

He brought the damp rag back to Marie and began to wipe off her face. Lucie seemed smugly content that he hadn't bothered to perform any similar service for her. She well knew a pitiful damp rag wasn't about to save any of them, anyway.

"I actually thought Pierre might be here," Marie said, laughing at the absurdity of ever holding out any such hope.

The smoke and steam continued to cause a thickening gray fog within the cove and beyond, further masking Isla Charlotte which, under normal conditions, would have been readily visible against the horizon.

"We're still alive," Charles reminded, offering the only consolation he could come up with at the moment. He guided Marie over to a large boulder and pulled her down with him beside it.

"Yes, we are still that, aren't we?" she admitted.

"Together, too," Charles reminded. "Don't forget that, either."

"How could I?" she said and cuddled deeper into her

husband's strong arms, preferring his animal warmth to the sickening heat that was taking full possession of the air all around them.

CHAPTER TEN
BIRDSONG

It was the sound of one bird, somewhere in the jungle, above the cove, that pierced Marie's subconscious and sucked her back to reality with a jolt.

For the birds had all left Saint-Georges, hadn't they? She had seen them go.

Her first emotion, upon fully waking, was shock that she had been asleep at all. How wasteful if she had spent her last hours of life dozing when she should have savored each and every precious moment she had remaining with the man she loved.

Next, flashed fear, in that Charles was gone. It was Lucie Bruay who stood over her.

The air was opaque with floating motes of dust that made the sun seem a Cyclops's eye obscured by milky cataracts. Mists swirled the surfaces of the water and the land.

"Your husband asked me to stay with you until you woke up, or until he got back," Lucie said.

The earth was still; the air was hot without being suffocating, and...there...were...more bird songs in the distance.

"So, when he gets back, you must tell him that I did what he asked, and have gone," Lucie said. Somewhere she had located the charred piece of tree limb that she used as a staff.

"Gone where?"

"While we have survived, others, I fear, haven't been nearly so fortunate," Lucie said. "I must give whatever help to them that I can."

Marie was tempted to throw it up in the old woman's face that, yes, they *were* alive, despite Lucie's continual prophesies of doom and gloom throughout the whole previous afternoon, evening, and night, but she held her tongue. There was too little to be gained by prematurely thumbing her nose at fate, especially if what had seemingly ended might not be ended at all.

"Fyrea can be a forgiving goddess," Lucie rationalized, possibly suspecting the thoughts, at that very moment, racing through Marie's head.

"Where is Charles?"

"Gone to look around. He said to tell you he won't be long."

"Shouldn't you at least wait until he gets back?"

"Why? What is done is done...for the moment."

Marie wondered how the women could possibly be so certain, especially since Lucie's foretelling of death for the three of them had so-far proven wrong.

Had it been wrong, though, only because of the magnanimity shown them by the goddess deity of the volcano?

Lucie started toward the pathway leading up the

slope, moving with considerable agility, considering her age and all she had been though. Before she reached the base of the bluff, however, she turned back.

"I know the properties of the plant *Digliji* very well," she said. "Your husband's spells will become less frequent. In time, they will cease entirely, leaving him free of any ties with which my daughter once sought to bind him."

"Thank you...for telling me that," Marie said.

"My daughter was a fool," Lucie said in a weary voice that relayed the full weight of her years. Her head began to shake; whether of her initiative, or because of an automatic spasm, was impossible for Marie to say.

The old woman turned and began her slow ascent of the hillside.

* * * * * * *

Marie didn't have fresh clothes but felt better, nevertheless, after stripping down to take a soapless bath in the surprisingly lukewarm water of the cove. Shortly after she was dressed, she heard Charles call from the top of the bluff. She scampered up the slope to meet him halfway, falling into his arms, and eagerly opening her hungry lips beneath the demanding pressure of his.

Oh, how she loved him!

Their kiss finally broken, he wrapped his right arm securely around her waist and helped her finish the climb to the top.

She glanced over an expanse of terrain with great smoldering swaths of denuded landscape where greenery had once grown.

"It's still standing?" she marveled, hardly believing the distant chimneys of Château Camaux seen through the mist.

"I imagine you're not too keen on still living there, after all of this," Charles said thoughtfully. "I've been thinking you might prefer we live in England."

"England?" Marie asked indignantly. "My home is wherever you are. If you think you married a woman who is scared by a few obstacles thrown in her way, you are sadly mistaken."

"You'd consider staying on Saint-Georges, then?" he asked, obviously surprised and delighted.

"You do want me to stay, don't you? I mean, you don't really want us to live in England, do you?"

"I want to live where you are...forever."

"Then, it's settled!" Marie gave her husband's muscled waist a tight squeeze. "So, let's go see what damage is done to our home, shall we?"

"In a minute," Charles said, turning Marie lovingly in his strong arms, kissing her eyes, her nose, her mouth, her throat....

Heat quickly possessed their bodies which was far more intense and all-consuming than anything which had ever yet raged within The Cauldron.

ABOUT THE AUTHOR

WILLIAM MALTESE, an international best-selling author of novels, short stories, including his popular Wildside Mystery Double, *Incident at Aberlene* and *Incident at Brimzinsky* (Spies & Lies #1-2), has published (under various pseudonyms) some 200 books in genres ranging from straight and gay erotica, mystery, romance, western, adventure, espionage, cooking, wine, young adults and children, and twenty-four science fiction/fantasy/horror novels, beginning with *Five Roads to Tlen* in 1969 (as "William J. Lambert III") through *Bond-Shattering* (2007). For a comprehensive list of his literary output, see *Draqualian Silk: A Collector's and Bibliographical Guide to The Books of William Maltese, 1969-2010* (Borgo Press, 2010). With a Business/Advertising degree, Maltese enlisted in the U.S. Army, where he achieved and was honorably discharged with the rank of Sergeant (E-5). You can find him at:

www.williammaltese.com
www.facebook.com/williammaltese
www.myspace.com/williammaltese
williammaltese@yahoo.com (e-mail)